BLOOD SLAVE

To Chloe,

Tasty stuff! ☺

Round Two

Eden Wildblood

By

Eden Wildblood

WARNING

Please note – This book is a dark paranormal story and is not suitable for those under 18 years old.

This book is dark. There will be moments you won't like and people you will hate. Know this before you go in...

ONE

Thud, thud, thud!

The strange apparition of the woman vanished as quickly as she had appeared, leaving Wynter alone in her office once again. She'd evidently chosen to come when all her hope was lost, and her thoughts were still reeling as she turned towards the doorway and frowned. Only this time, she wasn't sad or afraid any longer, but instead filled with determination. The odd woman had told her there was another option on the table. She didn't have to be turned, and wouldn't necessarily have to run either. All hope was not lost, after all. Or so she held onto that belief.

She continued to watch as the door was being pounded on so hard she thought it might be about to come off its hinges, and then began to panic. Was Marcus onto her and had come thundering down to put an end to the strange conversation she'd somehow just managed to have with a kind of spectre? Was she in trouble for not having gotten straight to work on time and instead been wallowing in self-pity? Wynter honestly didn't think anyone cared enough to come chasing her down for personal reasons, so figured it had to be him.

1

Her blood ran cold at the thought. And how different those feelings towards him suddenly were. The curse truly was lifted, and rather than feel any sort of pull in her vampire boss's direction, she wanted nothing more than to run away.

She forced herself to calm down and remember the promise the strange woman had given her. There was a way out, all she had to do was be patient, and so she unlocked the door and inched it open to find Warren glowering at her from the other side.

It was a relief to see him, in spite of the anger reddening his cheeks.

"What?" she hollered, and then let out a shriek when he barged his way inside and flung himself down onto the chair she had been sat crying in just minutes before.

"Lock the door, Wynter," he then demanded, and she watched as he rolled his sleeves up, showing off his extensive collection of tattoos, while also revealing fresh cuts on the inside of his wrists. So, he'd lost a fight in the end after all. Served him right.

Wynter didn't know why, but she was glad. Pleased to see that he'd had to whore himself out to the vampires in the end after all. Glad that after refusing to help her earlier that morning Warren had been forced to fight and had eventually lost. Even if his denial had apparently been because he had wanted something real, rather than a show for Marcus's amusement.

Did he regret denying her? He didn't seem to. In fact, he seemed to have regretted letting her get close to him at all.

She did as he had asked and locked them inside, but then turned back to him with her arms folded and a hard expression on her still tear-stained face. Two could play this game, and she'd had more than enough practice at being a frosty bitch over the years.

"What do you want?" she asked with an icy edge to her tone she knew she had to thank Marcus for. He'd taught her well, it seemed. "To help me? To protect me? Because, of course, I'm one of you. And you take care of your own…" she mocked, reminding him of his promises from before.

"I came by earlier and all I could hear was you crying, Wynter. It broke my heart to hear you that way. To know I had caused some of that pain when I left you behind and refused to help you. I'm sorry," he groaned in response, not even arguing back.

Warren suddenly looked lost. He seemed more than just hurt or tired, he looked broken.

The visions the Priestess had given her returned by force and she felt an ache rattle through her chest. Warren was going to end up either dead at her feet or running for his life if she chose him over Marcus. She hadn't seen the man's face in her second vision, but it had to be him. There was no one else she cared for enough to run from their oppressive master with. No one that mattered enough to try.

She knew she had to push him away. This couldn't get in the way of her plan to escape, and so she quickly realised she had to force him to back off. It was the only chance she had to save him. And potentially herself.

Wynter finally had options, albeit ones which were far from optimal. She could become a vampire and Marcus's immortal bride, which meant she'd gladly drain and kill even those she cared about, including the man sitting opposite her. Or she could run away and still risk their safety for her own selfish means. He hadn't lied when he'd told her who would die first for her foolishness, and Wynter knew there would have to be another way.

Which of course, there was also option number three now. To follow Marcus and let him lead her to the witch, as the woman who had appeared to her had stated. He would apparently take Wynter to her given a bit of time, and there she would be given an alternative to her either becoming a bloodsucker or a runaway.

She knew she'd do whatever it took to try for a future other to that in which she was Marcus's soul mate, and eventually did the unthinkable and murdered Warren. The only man who meant a thing to her. The one she had given her freedom up for. He didn't know it, but he was the only reason she was even still in Marcus's godforsaken club at all. She would've been long gone if he hadn't issued her with an ultimatum. Him or her freedom, but the price of it was Warren's life.

"I don't care about you, Warren," she lied, "I wasn't crying for you, but for me. I'm looking out for myself now. I'm not one of your friends or on your team. I'm your boss and as far as I'm concerned you can stay locked down in your basement day and night. I'll email you when I need an IT guy."

It broke her heart to say those words, but Wynter felt she had to. She knew he had been telling the truth about being sorry and that just made it hurt even more. Warren hadn't meant to upset her by saying no earlier that morning. He cared deeply for her and Wynter knew it, but so did Marcus. His adoration came with dangerous consequences for anyone who tried to get between the pair of them, and so her budding relationship with the burly geek had to be over. She would put an end to this before it even began because, if she were sacrificing her freedom to save his life, she would go one step further and also save him from a broken heart. Even if that meant her having to rip her own to shreds to find the strength to make it so.

"Sure. Whatever," he answered as he climbed back on to his feet. Warren then cracked his knuckles and stormed over to the door like the brute she'd always thought he was, but then he faltered at the last step. He turned back to her and showed the pain in his eyes as he took her in. He knew she didn't mean it, but seemed to agree that this was for the best for now, and so stayed silent as he finally ducked out of her office and disappeared into the night without so much as looking back again.

Wynter kept herself locked away all night long after she'd kicked Warren out. He called up an hour after having left and was clearly still raging, she could tell, and he somehow managed to convey using his tone of voice alone how he didn't believe her. That he was indeed the fighter she had seen in that ring and he wasn't going to back off. He was going to keep on coming for her.

Even more reason to follow the apparition's instructions and follow Marcus into whatever darkness he intended to lead her. She would play the game. Play nice.

She had to.

When two-am came around, she was out the door and heading up in the lift without hesitation. But this time, thanks to the lack of a hex dragging her to him by force, she decided it was her God-given right to have her say. Rather than throw herself at Marcus like she had the mornings previously, Wynter stormed over to him and slammed her hands down on the desk he had strewn her over on more than a couple of occasions.

"Good morning, Wynter," he told her with that bright, devious smile of his, "so wonderful to see you."

"Remove it," she growled, ignoring his greeting. Marcus's eyebrow flicked up in question, and Wynter saw it as a challenge rather than a show of his confusion. He was always completely in the know about his employees. Especially her—his new favourite. And she was a fighter too, just like Warren. That was what Marcus had said he so liked about her on more than one occasion and she was determined not to ever stop fighting him.

She unbuttoned her blouse and let it fall open,

ignoring the passion in his eyes as he swept his icy blue gaze over her exposed flesh. She had intended to show him her chest where the Priestess had touched her, placing some kind of spell on her.

"Ah if you're that eager for me to feed, you only needed to elaborate, my sweet," he told her as he stood and stalked around to her side of the desk. Then, with what appeared to be no effort at all, Marcus grabbed her by the shoulders, plucked Wynter off her feet like a child, and then deposited her on the wooden top.

She tried to fight him off but he was far too strong, of course. Marcus had her pinned down in an instant and he leaned over her, and she hated how helpless she was to stop him.

He then placed a gentle kiss against Wynter's lips, ignoring her writhing, before working his way down to her neck. There, he pressed his razor-sharp tongue down, which broke the skin over her artery, and a second later he began to drink.

Wynter felt her body rush with the usual endorphins that were a result of the feeding process. Like a bittersweet way of blocking out the gore and eliciting a carnal response, Marcus's bite still made her desirous for more, regardless of her having broken the curse he had placed her under the day he'd hired her. She was under an entirely different kind of spell when he fed and found she relaxed in a heartbeat. In spite of all her strength of will and desire for independence, she shoved her hands in his dark hair and pulled him closer, reacting to his deep gulps with moans and sighs of pleasure.

God damn it. She was torn all over again. Questions were running through her mind at an alarming rate, her head spinning with them.

Why couldn't she just stop all of this and walk away? Why did she have to be so foolish and not jump at the first chance she'd been given at a different life? Why did she have to enjoy Marcus this way? Enjoy his touch. His smell. The feel of him against her skin...

When he sealed the wound and lifted his head away, he grinned down at her, and Wynter found herself smiling back. She even stroked his stubble covered chin and let her body curl towards his, like he was some kind of a magnet.

"Marcus," she hissed, and clutched at the lapels of his wool jacket, keeping him close.

"Yes?" he whispered back, and then licked his lips clean of her blood.

The feeding was well and truly over though, and she snapped back to reality and remembered what she'd come in demanding.

"Tell your witch to remove her locator spell, or so help me God I'll..."

"You'll what, fight her? She'd crush you like a bug, Wynter. You could try and run of course, but that wouldn't end well," he teased, laughing to himself as she shoved him away.

However, Marcus did focus his gaze on the exact spot Wynter had felt the Priestess mark her and he looked thoughtful for a moment, as though considering her request. "The locator spell remains intact until I can trust you not to run from me."

She let out an angry shriek and sat up, and then proceeded to button her blouse back up in a bid to hide her body from him. She'd even worn trousers, just for the occasion, so she could keep his prying hands at bay, and so curled her legs up and sat with them crossed in front of her.

"What's it gonna take?" she then asked, and Marcus positively beamed at her readiness to negotiate.

"Your soul," he replied, before tilting her back down and then ripping her trousers clean off her legs and waist. He had his mouth over the vein on her thigh a second later and Wynter quickly felt herself falling under his mesmerising spell before she could stop him, not that she thought she could if she wanted to. However, his words rung in her head and she remembered the warning from the strange apparition she'd seen in her office. If a vampire's soul merged with a human's then they were done for. Bonded for life. If he did so with her, Wynter would be done for too.

She peered down her half-naked body and frowned at the man lapping at her vein. However of course, he was no man at all, but a monster. One whom she despised. And yet, Marcus had also been gentle at times. He had made her feel protected and comfortable, and had let her orgasm, even though all the others she had met had told her it was forbidden.

She was in complete and utter turmoil, but he didn't seem to care. All he wanted was his satisfaction, and she was about to beg him to stop feeding so she could keep some of her strength, when his hand reached up her opposite thigh and began caressing her sensitive flesh.

He crept higher and before Wynter could make a sound, Marcus had pushed aside her flimsy knickers and was stroking his way inside her molten core. Shit! She wasn't ready for that and let out a garbled moan, feeling beyond ready for more. She opened her thighs and arched her hips, eliciting a laugh from her predatory master.

Marcus continued to push his long fingers in and out, and it wasn't long before she felt the usual tension building within her that signified her impending orgasm. It was all too much. The bite and his wonderful touch all at once wasn't something she could fight, not that she wanted to. Not really.

She tried to stop it. Tried to call to him to stop feeding as she was so close, but it was no use. The orgasm burst forth and she shuddered with bliss as the wave overcame her, her body writhing against Marcus's fingers greedily as he continued to take her. She initially sought a second climax thanks to his relentless probing but, in a moment of clarity, opened her eyes to check whether Marcus was in a feeding frenzy or not. If he were, the best thing she could do was scream bloody murder and hope someone would come and pry his mouth from her vein before it was too late.

But instead, she was already safe. He had closed the wound without her realising and was watching her with a bloody smile. His gaze then lifted to hers and she saw his bright blue eyes seem to radiate with light from within. It was mesmerising.

Wynter stared into them, and imagined how if they switched off the lights in the room they would undoubtedly still shine like two icy beacons, and was about to laugh, when she remembered the reason why they shone like that. His soul, or whatever remained of it, was calling to hers, and she had to refuse it, or else.

"Marcus, your eyes," she whimpered, and then cried out when he yanked her off the desk and sat on his chair, pulling her onto his lap so she straddled him. His fingers continued their exploration between them and her body couldn't help but remain so ready for his touch. He coaxed her further towards her coveted second climax, and she was desperate for it, albeit utterly foolishly.

Wynter rode his hand like a woman possessed and she kissed Marcus with reckless abandon while doing so. She could taste her blood on his lips and knew it ought to disgust her, but she felt beyond all of that now. All she cared about was herself and the needs she too had to satisfy.

She felt like she might finally be succumbing to the cold nature she had pretended to have, and had Marcus to thanks for that. He had taught her a trick or two about being selfish, and so she took a second orgasm from him without asking or begging. It was empowering, and probably the hottest dose of foreplay she had ever received in her life.

9

As she came down, Marcus let his hands retreat. He even covered her back over with her soaked knickers and watched her with his usual smile, but with an extra glint in his still luminescent eyes.

"Do you have any idea how much I want you, Wynter?" he growled as he pressed her body against his. She could feel his raging hard-on beneath her and let out a laugh.

"Yeah, I think I do," she replied, "but you can't, can you? Not unless you want to merge your soul with mine."

Marcus seemed surprised that she could possibly know so much, but he didn't say so. He just offered her a nod before standing up and letting her feet fall to the floor. Wynter then watched as the light emanating from his eyes began to wane and by the time she had gathered her composure, it was gone completely.

Their moment was over, and she felt odd in the aftermath. The hex he had put her under a week previously might have been broken, but his bite still brought forth feelings that neither of them wanted to address once it was over.

Wynter felt awkward and still ever so confused. She wasn't sure what to say or do, so scooped up her ripped clothes and tossed them in the bin and then started walking towards the glass panel that partitioned the huge room. "I'm going to take a shower."

Marcus said nothing to stop her, and so she left without another word.

TWO

Marcus waited until Wynter was safely out of the way before summoning his Priestess. She appeared within seconds and kept her head bowed in respect beneath her shrouding hood and cape. He couldn't see a single piece of flesh beneath the red cloak, and not even her long auburn hair was billowing out like she sometimes wore it.

"My lady," he said in greeting.

"My lord," she answered, "what might I do for you?"

"Well, you can start by telling me why you decided to place a locator spell on our dear Wynter?" he replied, and knew there was a snide edge to his tone, but didn't rectify it. Marcus had hardly shouted at or had to raise his voice to his Priestess before, but when it came to his new favourite, he was ready to do whatever it took to ensure she remained his.

The Priestess had gotten close to her though. She had made love to her as he'd drunk from Wynter's vein. She had kissed and fondled her. Tasted that glorious body and elicited orgasms while having plenty of her own. Marcus knew it had been odd, the Priestess coming forward for such an explorative task, but she had. And, in the form of her usual guise, Marcella, she and Wynter had sparked quite a connection. One Marcus hoped was for his benefit, and not his Priestess's.

"I don't trust her," the witch answered. She had always been honest with Marcus, often brutally so, and he had no reason not to believe her still, so he waited for her to elaborate further before he spoke again. "She will return to you each night and remain here the three days you've agreed, but I do not believe she will have your interests at heart in the days between. I have seen numerous visions of her future. Some catastrophic. Others wondrous. I do not know for sure which path Wynter will take, but I am certain I must keep watch."

"And will you take action should I need you to?" Marcus demanded, stepping closer. He gave her some credit, she did not step away. Not even when he was so close he could hear her heart pounding in her chest.

"Always," she answered honestly, "and I will watch her on your behalf, my lord. I shall guide her to do your bidding and remain loyal."

"Then how is it she knows about the merging?" Marcus bellowed, his hand shooting up to her throat. Again, his Priestess did not back away. He felt nothing but her servitude and steadfast loyalty emanating from her and she even lifted her hands to remove the hood shrouding her face.

Her deep brown eyes drank him in and Marcus yanked his hand away from her neck as if it had been burned. He then placed it upon her cheek with a gentle hold. "Tell me why you showed her."

"She is entitled to see, just as you are, what the future holds. I showed her but two potential outcomes of your liaison. The first was the one I hope for the most."

"A future in which our souls have merged and she has been turned?"

"Of course. I will perform her ceremony myself."

Jealousy flooded through him and Marcus had to fight the urge to lash out at his Priestess again. Did she want that solely so she too could remain by Wynter's side? Did she have plans to steal her away and keep her for herself?

Marcus went to open his mouth to ask, when she cut him off. "Stop this charade, my lord. You want her, so take her. None of this is for my own personal desire. Wynter is yours and yours alone, but only if you accept your fate."

"And what of the lover you warned me she would choose over me?" he growled.

"A *male* of merit, my lord. Not I, nor any other female. Be warned, should their souls merge, you will forever regret it."

His Priestess then bowed and left him, leaving Marcus seething.

Warren. It had to be him. No one else had turned Wynter's head. Not a single human had made her feel anything more than passing attraction. Not David. Not even Marcella. But with that burly geek, Wynter was a bundle of mixed emotions. He'd been able to sense them himself and knew the feelings were mutual. Warren wanted her too, but the foolish boy didn't know that she had given up her freedom for his sake, and Wynter had made him swear to it that he never would.

That didn't mean he couldn't toy with him though.

Marcus left the office before Wynter had even emerged from her shower. He trusted that she'd stay there and use the time for a well-earned rest, and so headed down to the same club floor he had taken her to the previous day. His clients were lining up at the ready for their feeds, and each nodded to him respectfully as he passed. Some reeled with admiration for his stature, while others were envious, perhaps even violently so. He simply smiled. They could try and overthrow him if they so pleased. Marcus had thwarted many a foe over the years and of course, more arose with every passing decade. Their kind all wanted power. They craved it over their prey and coveted it in their everyday lives. Marcus was one of the only vampires who made a fortune feeding them, while not having to pay a single penny for his own Blood Slaves. He was master of all that he saw, and then some.

He was also clever and cunning. He had files regarding the lives of every vampire in his extensive list of clients, and would find ways to bring them down should they so much as try to rise up against him.

But not today. Right now, there was only one person he wanted to bring down. He knew where he wanted to go. To the same ring as before, and to the same slave.

"Mr Cole, what a pleasant surprise," one of his burly human guards said in greeting. He had a device in his palm that held the timetable for the day's bookings, and Marcus put his hand out for it. It was the man's and the other day staffs' job to oversee the successful deliverance of the slaves for his kind to feed from, and they had been briefed never to relinquish the device to any vampire, all except him. Many of his kind coveted their technology, and so the guards themselves were warded. Their blood was poison and if any vampire took so much as one drop, they would die a slow and painful death that no witch on Earth could provide an antidote to. It was his safeguard, and yet the boy had handed it over to his ruthless ruler without hesitation. He knew better than to argue with the master of his fate, after all.

Marcus grinned and peered down at the list. Today was Warren's lucky day. He had two vampire opponents lined up for later that morning, followed by a nice big gap so that he could rest. Well, that wasn't going to happen. In fact, he was going to need the rest sooner than anticipated because Marcus had plans for him.

"Send Warren down now," he barked, and the guard

relayed the message via radio to the team who looked after the slaves on the first floor of the club.

He arrived just minutes later and approached the pair of them with a frown.

"Mr Cole?" he said, and was right to be uneasy. "Has an extra fight been added?" Marcus nodded and then ushered Warren towards the boxing ring. He climbed in and went over to his corner, and then silence fell as Marcus climbed up after him.

"Yes, little rabbit," he taunted him while wearing his most wicked of smiles. "I told you you're my new favourite, didn't I? So let's have some fun together."

Marcus removed his jacket and unbuttoned his shirt.

"Sir, I can't fight you," Warren pleaded, but Marcus continued to prepare. When he was ready, he stepped into the centre of the ring and used his power over Warren to lure him closer.

"Try," Marcus whispered with a bright smile, even though he knew it would be torture for Warren to do so. "Try for me. For your wounded pride. For Wynter and everything I have stolen from her..."

They were nose-to-nose and yet still, Warren refused to strike, so Marcus threw the first punch. With a blow strong enough to break a lesser man in two, he sent the boy flying backwards into the ropes, where he crumbled into a heap and curled into a ball on the floor of the ring.

Marcus grinned, but found he wasn't all that satisfied. The hex was too strong. He wouldn't fight back, not unless the Priestess lifted it, and Marcus wasn't about to go that far just to get a good fight out of him.

Delivering him with a good beating would have to do instead. He summoned Warren back to him again and then rained down blows upon him, leaving him covered in blood and bruises, but still breathing. Still alive. For now.

***

Strangely, Wynter wasn't tired after her shower. She got changed into one of the horrendous frilly nightdresses Marcus always stocked and gave her scruffy hair a few scrunches into messy waves, and then she padded out into the office but found he had left her alone. She wasn't expecting that, so thought for a minute what she could do to pass the time. Marcus wasn't exactly the type of guy to have books at the ready or a television, so she decided she'd go down to her office instead and retrieve her handbag so she could catch up with her friends via her mobile phone. She'd only be gone a few minutes and wouldn't leave the building so figured it'd be okay.

Wynter was as quick as possible. In and out in a minute, but still made sure to properly lock her office behind her on the way back out to the lift. She was just finishing up when she turned and found David watching her from down the hall. He had a sort of smug smile that made a shiver creep down her spine. And that was the perfect word for how he was coming across—like some sort of creep.

He approached at speed and Wynter groaned and moved as quickly as she could for the elevator. There, she hit the call button and then lifted a hand in an attempt to stop him from getting any nearer.

"Not now, David," she tried when that didn't work. What happened to their agreement to put things between them on hold and remain friends? He came to a stop just beside the lift and when she climbed inside, he wedged his foot in the way of the sensor to stop the doors closing behind her. "Please, I need to get back upstairs," she begged, hugging her body in an attempt to cover up. Damn, she wished she'd gotten changed into something more appropriate than just the nightdress. It was thin enough that he could probably see right through it, and the last thing she wanted was for David to still believe he might have a chance with her.

"What were you doing? Sneaking around?" he asked her with a snide edge to his tone. So, all niceties were clearly out of the window now that she had given him the brush off all week, but she wasn't going to let him upset her. She'd dealt with creeps before, and scowled up at him in the same way she always did with those who'd tried it on with her in the past.

"In my own office?" she retorted, and added an eye roll. "Gimmie a fucking break."

David laughed her remark off and then actually seemed to relax a little. He still had both hands either side of the elevator door though, blocking it entirely, and he leaned back and looked up and down the corridor behind him. It appeared as if he might be about to walk away, but then he apparently changed his mind. A dark look swept across his face as an idea seemed to come to him.

Using his grip on the frame, David propelled himself into the elevator with Wynter and he had her pinned to the wall behind in a second, licking his lips while staring down into her face. This wasn't what she wanted. Not in the slightest. Being stuck down an otherwise empty corridor in a lift that was about to take them up to a just as empty office was not what she'd ever imagined could happen. Not on Marcus's watch. But, it seemed this was happening, and when the lift began to ascend, Wynter panicked.

David's boyish charm was gone. The soft and tender way he'd had with her at first was long forgotten. All that remained was a predator, and one who she didn't particularly feel like entertaining the advances of. "Back off, David. Give me some space."

"I did," he growled and then pressed himself even tighter against her, invading Wynter's personal space on more than just an overbearing level, but a dangerous one. "I left you alone all week and instead of you getting your shit together, you just grew closer to him," David added, pointing upwards. She knew the gesture meant Marcus, and she wanted to laugh at the sheer stupidity of the man. Everything she and their vampire boss shared had been thanks to his hex. Even now, their only tender moments were because of the affect his bite had on her, and she knew there was no real love between them. There probably never would be. "But you owe me, Wynter. I took care of you, now it's time you took care of me—"

He then gripped her hands and held them by her head as he lunged for her, kissing her roughly while prodding her with his rock hard cock in the belly. Wynter tried to fight him off, but he was stronger than she'd imagined, and by the time the lift arrived on the fourth floor, she was firmly in his grasp.

David emerged, holding her by the throat, and he looked around, clearly checking to see if Marcus was lurking there. He was still gone, and Wynter cursed him for being absent. The one time she needed him and he was nowhere to be found. Go figure.

"He'll kill you for this," she spat, but David didn't seem to care.

He flung her face down onto the rough carpet floor and lifted her flimsy nightgown to reveal her nakedness beneath. Wynter kicked and screamed against his roving hands, trying desperately to fend him off, but he just held her down by the back of the neck and pressed her cheek against the hard ground.

She couldn't move.

She could hardly even breathe, and cried out when the realisation hit that there was nothing she could do to stop him from doing whatever the hell he wanted to next.

But then, he was gone. His harsh hold on her suddenly absent. Not just let go, but ripped away as

David was plucked from atop her by force. It was as if some kind of giant hand, like a grabber in one of those arcade games at the beach, had ripped him up into the air and taken him away.

Wynter was sure it had to be Marcus having come to her aid at last, and she clambered up onto her knees and scooted forward so she could get out of their way. Trembling, she scrambled over by the wall and tucked herself into a ball as she tried to hide and block out what would surely be about to ensue, but then all she could hear was the thumping of her heart in her ears. Nothing else. No fight. No telling off. Just, nothing...

When she eventually lifted her head and peered around to try and figure out what was happening, David was no longer there, but neither was Marcus. And it didn't appear to be some cruel joke or a ploy from David to make her think the ordeal was over. He genuinely had been removed from the situation, or so it seemed.

A garbled groan then alerted her senses again and Wynter began to whimper. Of course he couldn't have disappeared entirely, and she began looking around for any sign of him, but there was nothing.

"Help... please," then came a clearer groan, and Wynter finally managed to follow the sound. She peered up and found David at last. Like something out of a horror movie, he was stuck to the high ceiling right above where he'd just been holding her down moments before. That was the only way she could describe it. He was lying flat against the dark ceiling tiles against all laws of gravity, and looked like he was being crushed up into them by force. Wynter whimpered and gazed up at him, but she didn't move or try to help him. All she could do was stare in absolute horror.

David had to have been propelled up there by some serious force. He was bleeding from his ears and nose thanks to the impact to the back of his head, plus his right leg was bending the wrong way, clearly broken. He had to be in so much pain, but she had no idea what to do, or whether she was capable of doing anything at all. Or if she even wanted to.

He opened his mouth like he was going to plead for help again, when he suddenly went flying back down to the ground with an almighty crack, as though whatever forces holding him up had let go just as suddenly as when they'd first grabbed him.

Wynter heaved at the sight, and knew the awful cracking sound she'd heard had to have been that of more of bones breaking, and she full on gagged at the sight of his crumpled body laying still on the ground. Her instinct was to rush to his aid, and yet there was another voice echoing through her skull. One that told her to let the son of a bitch die. That he deserved it.

She made a lame attempt to sit up and move toward him, as though that would make her feel better about wanting to leave him to die. As if she could convince herself she'd tried and how her conscience was clear.

Before she could move another inch though, David was launched back up to the ceiling, but he didn't remain there. A second later, he plummeted back down, and so on. It was as if he were inside a box that someone was shaking. Up and down his body flew, crushing a bit more with each impact, and Wynter could do nothing but watch in horror as his life slowly drained from him.

When he was nothing but a broken mess, the rattling finally stopped, as did his punishment. Silence descended and Wynter clambered backwards as far as she could. She didn't stop until she was sat against the far wall and there, she shook back and forth, unable to take her eyes off the bloody mess before her.

"That's what the locator spell was for, my love," the deep, resonating voice of the Priestess then chimed from across the room, and Wynter looked up to find the cloaked woman standing at the open end of the glass wall. She was covered from head to toe, like before, so Wynter couldn't see her face, but she somehow knew the strange woman was smiling. She was pleased with herself, and Wynter couldn't even begin to understand the mind of someone who'd think nothing of taking a life so violently.

"You sensed I was in danger?" she mumbled, thinking about what the Priestess had just said.

"Yes…"

"So you killed him?" she cried in a shrill tone, her throat closing up as she tried to breathe and fight back her tears.

Shock was clearly setting in, and Wynter felt herself trembling harder. The cold was seeping into her bones through her thin nightgown. Invading her, just like David had wanted to do. And just like the Priestess had successfully done with her spell.

"Yes…" the witch replied, "you can thank me later."

Wynter began laughing hysterically, which then turned to tears and wailing sobs. She couldn't speak, but knew there were no words to convey how sickened she felt.

The Priestess simply stood and watched her come undone, and didn't try to engage her or come closer so as to offer any form of comfort or apology. She simply observed her for a few seconds before disappearing back into the nothingness.

A blink of her eye and the woman was gone, and Wynter was immediately aware of how she was stuck in Marcus's office with no one but a bloody and pretty much unidentifiable corpse to keep her company.

She opened her mouth and let out a blood-curdling scream. The loudest, most painful shriek she had ever cried before. She didn't stop until she was hoarse and delirious with shock.

But then, she was acutely aware of a pair of strong

arms picking her up off the floor and holding her close. Someone was shushing her and sharing their warmth to help soothe her, and it felt amazing.

Wynter was so glad not to be alone with David any longer that she clung to her saviour harder, expecting it to be Marcus, but when she peered up into his face, she found the hard set of a different man's jaw. His was chiselled and strong, and beautiful. She saw blond hair instead of his dark grey, and then the most incredible grey-blue eyes that locked on hers and held them.

"It's okay," the man told her in a heavily accented voice, "we can take care of 'dis."

THREE

The elevator then arrived with a *ding* and Wynter felt the air in the room suddenly go ice cold. It was as if someone had just turned on the air conditioning full blast, and every inch of her went back to being frozen. She knew it was Marcus and could sense his rage emanating out of him in waves, but for whatever reason, he wasn't making a show of force against the man holding her. And he wasn't running over to release her from his grip.

The room was silent and still, everything at a standstill, as if time itself had stopped. Wynter knew she had to do something, and so tried to wriggle out of the grasp still holding her tightly. It was no use. The man just pressed her harder against him.

"What is the meaning of this, Jakob?" Marcus shouted, and her odd saviour stopped dead. He didn't so much as draw a breath, and after a second, he seemed to decide on his course of action.

The man holding her turned and as he did, Wynter could see Marcus properly at last. His gaze locked on hers and her stomach lurched. Was he angry with her for accepting the strange man's help? Did he blame her for what had happened to David? She couldn't read him at all, but knew one thing for sure. She was going to be in some serious trouble if she didn't get away from the man who had scooped her into his arms. Jakob, or so Marcus had called him. The name sounded foreign, which matched his accent. Perhaps Russian?

"While you were distracted, your slave was attacked, old friend. It's a good thing your Priestess arrived in time to save her," Jakob replied in that same accented tone, his voice deep and gruff. It was alluring, and she stared up into his face again. He really was an admirable sight, and the lack of emotion on his face only made her more attracted to him.

Jeez, she really did have a type. And a hell of a lot of issues.

Wynter shook it off, figuring it was just another vampire and their captivating way they had about them. The magic lure they had that made you go willingly towards death. He would undoubtedly drink her dry given half the chance, just like the rest of them.

Marcus stepped closer to the pair of them, but didn't seem in any rush to come and get her. Maybe he was proving to his guest that he was still in control and so didn't need to fight him. Or maybe the message was to her. Either way, she could tell the gory scene he'd just found in his office had mystified him. Wynter guessed he had been expecting to find it empty of all but her once he returned, and yet he'd walked in to find her in the arms of another vampire while another of his blood slaves lay dead on the ground.

"I knew my Priestess would handle things in my absence," Marcus replied with an air of nonchalance Wynter almost believed, if it weren't for the remarkable chill still lingering in the air between them. He then put out his hand, his palm up. "Come, Wynter," he told her, as if she was still under his spell and he was summoning her to him. As though he still had the power to force her movements.

She knew she had to play along. To pretend she was still hexed. For whatever reason, Jakob had to think she was beholden to Marcus for purposes other than bribery and forced submission, and so Wynter gave it all she had to try and wriggle free from his hold.

With a huff, he finally let her clamber out of his grasp, and Wynter made for Marcus as quickly as her shaky legs could take her. She was sure to go in a large arc around the crumpled body still lying in a heap in the centre of the office, his blood now dark and congealed. David's face was almost unrecognisable and Wynter had to look away from the awful sight or else she had a feeling she might be sick.

She focused instead on Marcus's outstretched hand and ran the last few steps to take it and let him pull her to him. Wynter tucked herself under his arm and tried to focus solely on him, but then she turned her face and caught Jakob staring at her.

He was too intense. Too knowing. He was watching her with a look that said he was reading her like a book, and she didn't like it one little bit.

Marcus bristled and held Wynter closer. "Please take a seat, Jakob. Allow me a moment to settle my slave and I'll be right with you."

Without waiting for the go ahead, Marcus then led Wynter away and behind the glass partition. With her still tucked under his arm, he took her into the bathroom and then held her at arm's length, eyeing her up and down.

"I'm s-sorry," she mumbled, looking down at her nightdress that was covered in dirt and blood from her altercation with David. Wynter knew Marcus liked her clean, but now she felt more than just dirty. She felt broken. All she could picture when she closed her eyes was David's face, and the dark look on it as he'd eyed her and forced himself into her personal space. She could still feel his hands on her, and a shudder echoed down her spine.

"Take it off," Marcus answered with a frown, and she immediately did as she was told. "Did he hurt you?" he then asked and Wynter nodded. "Where?"

She showed him her neck and the friction burns to her knees and elbows. Marcus said nothing as he then inspected her body thoroughly, checking each bruise and scrape David had given her. He even parted her thighs to check he hadn't caused any damage there, and seemed satisfied enough that she was still in one piece and hadn't been violated. "Get washed up and dressed, and then get some rest. I'll be back shortly."

Marcus then turned to leave, but Wynter grabbed his hand. He twisted and scowled at her, but she refused to back down and stared into his eyes pleadingly.

"Please don't leave me," she implored.

Marcus's eyes flashed with that iridescent brightness at her plea, but he seemed lost for words. Wynter used the silence to her advantage and stepped closer to him, nestling her cold and naked body against his before planting a soft kiss against his pursed lips. "Please, Marcus. Stay."

"No," he eventually groaned before gently pushing her away.

Wynter knew he had to get back to his guest, but the rejection aroused venomous feelings from within her and she lashed out. She slapped Marcus as hard as she could manage and then tried for a second one, but he was too quick. He grabbed her flying hand and stopped it with ease, and then frowned down at her through hooded eyes. "You get one, Wynter. Don't push it. Trust me, if David wasn't already dead, I'd have him strung up so I could butcher him slowly. Take pleasure in his pain and torment. And all in vengeance for his crimes against you, my sweet."

A sob burst from her chest and Wynter shook her

head franticly as she crumbled once again.

"Liar," she cried, "you don't care about me." She then wrenched out of his grip and stumbled away, catching herself just before she went crashing into the glass door to the shower cubicles.

"Yeah, keep telling yourself that if you think it'll help," Marcus retorted before heading for the door.

"Fuck off," Wynter croaked, but then her heart sank when he opened the door and did exactly that.

By the time she'd cleaned herself up, Wynter was already a lot calmer, but she still hated the idea of being alone. She'd been in the bathroom a while and hoped to God that Marcus's meeting with the strange and yet enigmatic Jakob was over so she didn't have to be on her own once she was back out in the living space behind the office.

She emerged in just a towel and went to the dresser, expecting to find another old-style nightie there, but instead she found black leggings and a fluffy jumper with stars painted on it. They were just like the ones she wore to bed at home in her cold house and Wynter climbed into them both with a soppy smile. This was much better than the old fashioned nightgowns Marcus had insisted she wear before. Warmth immediately spread through her and Wynter felt tired at last. In fact, she was exhausted.

She went over to the sofa and sat on it, listening for any sign of Marcus and Jakob around the corner. She could hear them talking, however the conversation was too muffled for her to make out. But at least Marcus was there. He was close by. She pulled her knees up and hugged them, willing sleep to come, but it didn't. She was just too on edge. Too wired.

She stood and began to pace up and down in a bid to expel her nervous energy, and was about to give up and run for the elevator when the Priestess appeared out of nowhere and blocked her path.

"Come," her deep voice whispered, and the witch held out her gloved hand. Wynter refused to take it though. She was still wary of the strange woman, even after she'd saved her. Especially after that. Her chosen method was not what Wynter would've ever had in mind.

"Where?" she demanded, earning herself a laugh of amusement.

"To sleep," the Priestess then answered, but she dropped her hand and instead went to the couch, where she sat and nestled herself against one of the corners to get comfortable. She then placed one of the pillows on her lap and patted it gently.

"Just sleep?" Wynter asked, but she was already moving towards her anyway. Already succumbing to her tiredness and the deep-seated sense of trust she somehow had towards the strange woman. Something about the Priestess made Wynter want to be near her. Want to touch her. It was like they were already part of one another. As if they had shared more than just a few fleeting moments together. Wynter couldn't put her finger on why, but she was already beginning to feel like she knew her.

"I'll protect you, my love. Watch over you," the Priestess insisted, and Wynter climbed down on the sofa, fighting a yawn as she went. She then put her head on the pillow and closed her eyes, and couldn't deny she felt calmer than she had a few minutes earlier. Sleep was taking her, and Wynter let it.

She felt safe, kind of like her guardian angel was watching over her. The woman who had protected her from an attacker. The one who was there when Marcus had refused her. It didn't matter whether she agreed with her methods or not, what mattered was that the Priestess had been there for her when it counted. Even if she'd never seen her face, she was still the closest thing she had to a friend right now.

"Thank you," she whispered, and then let herself fall into a deep and dreamless sleep.

***

The pleasantries and small talk over, Marcus turned to Jakob and got down to business. He'd had enough playing nice and knew it was time they were honest with each other about why the dangerous and somewhat unpredictable vampire assassin had turned up at his club unannounced. He wasn't here of his own accord, Marcus knew that much at least, and so he fixed him with a knowing stare.

"So, she sent you to spy on me?" he asked, and Jakob nodded. They both knew who he was on about. Jakob's employer, Camilla. "And you came. You saw. Time to relay back about what I've been up to and why I've ignored her invitations to spend an evening with her. But then you showed yourself rather than slink away unnoticed. Why?"

Jakob's lip curled into a knowing smile, and it was all Marcus could do not to reach over and slap the guy. He'd been right. Jakob had been slinking around unannounced and hadn't intended on showing himself. It wasn't hard to figure out why.

"I 'vas intrigued by your slave. That man desired her so much he was willing to do whatever it took to have her. I could smell his desperation a mile away, and your Priestess isn't much better. She wants her. And so do you." Jakob then rubbed his strong chin thoughtfully and readily revealed what was on his mind. "She has you all ensnared. Don't think I cannot see your affection for her," he told him, and Marcus didn't deny it.

He couldn't lie, especially not to a skilled interrogator such as Jakob. It was the assassin's job to figure people out. To spot the truth and catch his prey in their lies.

And it was true. Wynter sure did have them all tied up in knots around her little finger. Thank God she didn't realise it, otherwise they would have a real issue with who was in control here. Marcus would be forced to show her it was him, and deep down, he didn't actually want to offer her his firm hand. He wanted to protect Wynter. To care for her. To *love* her…

No, he told himself. To love meant being weak, and that would never happen.

"And so what if the girl does have us spellbound? Her presence here is solely to feed me and entertain me, which she's doing a good job of. I don't see what business it is of yours, or your employer's?" he snapped.

Jakob shook his head, laughing to himself, and then he regarded Marcus with a smile.

"She gets jealous. You know 'dat. You've never given her a reason to be jealous before, but now all of a sudden you refuse to accept her invitation for an audience. Camilla simply wished to know why."

He didn't believe that for a single moment. She had to be more than just jealous to send Jakob after him.

"Indeed, and yet she and I have had the same arrangement for hundreds of years. Neither one of us forces the other to tend to their carnal needs. It is a mutually pleasurable affair, and one neither of us can claim to be exclusive or binding. Should I wish to refuse her and never take her to my bed again, I can without explanation. Please remind your boss of that," he countered.

"Surely you are not foolish enough to believe you mean nothing to her? To think she will let you go without a fight?" Jakob asked, but they both knew Marcus was neither a fool nor someone's boy-toy. He would take Camilla down in a heartbeat if he needed to and wouldn't so much as break a sweat in the process. But of course, that was exactly why an ancient vampire such as Camilla would have an assassin in her employ. A ruthless, cunning killer with no conscience and no soul, who would do his research well and find a way to end Marcus for her. She wouldn't even need to get her own hands dirty. Jakob had been her puppet for hundreds of years and while Marcus was still sure he would win in any fight, he knew one with him would be lengthy, bloody, and costly.

Jakob was notorious in his world. So famed for his retched way of life that vampires and all manner of magical creatures knew his face in every corner of the world. If he arrived in town, they all knew someone was about to die, and just had to hope it wasn't their name on his list.

He'd torn apart entire families before finally ripping out his true target's heart. He'd broken apart souls that had been merged for decades, killing both parties in the process. And then there had been the business with the village he had laid waste to simply because their leader had offended him by cheating in a game of poker. Such violence in his wake. Such chaos. And all without an ounce of guilt. No shame in what he had done or the legacy of nought but anarchy and death Jakob would undoubtedly leave behind.

Marcus wasn't willing to risk a war with him simply because his jilted lover had decided to take his dismissal badly. He knew an alternative had to be arranged. Or at the least, he would need to negotiate.

"Perhaps you should step up in my place, Jakob? You've remained loyal to Camilla for a long time and yet, as far as I can tell, have never been rewarded with more than your usual fee for serving her. Makes one wonder if there's something more than just your loyalty keeping you bound to her?"

Jakob frowned but didn't answer. He simply remained stoic, but he still bristled angrily and his reaction made Marcus wonder if he might be right. Maybe the heartless assassin was indeed a lover as well as a fighter. "You have seen for yourself how busy I am with my work. Tell Camilla I send my apologies, but I shan't be visiting with her again."

"You have a new lover in her place. Understood," Jakob snapped, and now it was Marcus's turn to have to hold back his anger.

How dare he presume that something sexual was going on between him and Wynter? Jakob had no place there with them and Marcus was quick to tell him so.

"Speculating will only make you look weak. Like a gossiping little woman deciding on stirring up trouble where there isn't any. I took you for better than that, old friend…"

Jakob rose to the challenge. He stood and fixed Marcus with a venomous stare.

"I 'vill tell Camilla you are indisposed. You can explain the rest to her yourself when she pays you a visit, which we both know will be her next approach. Thank you for your hospitality," Jakob answered, his voice robotic and forcibly calm.

"Farewell," Marcus answered, and then he watched as Jakob disappeared into the night via the open window at the other end of the room, rather than the door.

He inwardly cursed the highly trained soldier for being able to come and go as he damn well pleased, and then locked the place up tight. Marcus also checked every inch of his office, and he made a decision then and there to hire some more guards. Not humans this time, but something more on the same level as Jakob. Something powerful enough to hold him off, should the day come that the assassin came to visit for reasons other than to check up on him at Camilla's behest.

When he was satisfied that his fortress was clear and he and his minions were alone again, Marcus headed into the back of the huge office, and he let out a contented sigh when he found his Priestess still watching over Wynter as she slept.

He'd hated having to leave her, especially when she had begged him not to go, but had been forced to keep up appearances for Jakob's—and ultimately Camilla's—sake. The assassin couldn't know how his soul had yearned to comfort hers in her moment of need. How desperate he'd been to stay with her. And how heart breaking it had been to have to walk away.

It'd already been abundantly clear how horrendous he felt when he'd returned to find her in Jakob's arms after the attack. He could've cut the tension in the air with a goddamn knife, and it'd taken everything he had not to storm across the room and forcibly remove her from the assassin's grasp. And so, he'd had forced himself to pretend. To act as though he cared not for the woman herself but only for the blood in her veins he'd rightfully claimed, and was glad she'd figured him out and played along when he'd pretended to summon her back to his side. Such a clever girl, even when in shock following her awful traumatic experience.

He was also pleased to see that Marcella had taken it upon herself to fulfil the role of protector for him. There was no better person for the job. He knew that now. No one he trusted with Wynter's safekeeping more than his Priestess, and he vowed never to let himself feel jealous of her ever again.

His poor girl was curled in on herself protectively when he went to them. She had her head in the witch's lap, and she looked so peaceful it made his heart ache harder.

Marcus joined the pair of them on the sofa, having opted to squeeze on it by Wynter's side rather than take up one of the many other empty seats. He didn't explain himself nor did he feel he had to, and the Priestess didn't say a word. She was still shrouded, concealing her face, but he knew she wasn't asleep. Like him, she never slept.

After a few minutes of silence Marcus reached down and lifted Wynter's cold feet into his lap and frowned. Even in her fluffy pyjamas she was still frozen. She needed somewhere proper to sleep when she came to him. A bed with a warm blanket made up only for her. Just for his special slave.

He rubbed the warmth back into them and then sighed. It was time he found out exactly what had transpired that afternoon between her and David.

"Did he rape her?" he whispered into the silence.

"No, but he tried," the Priestess answered. Marcus had thought as much, but he needed to know for sure. He had purposely put David in Wynter's path, after all, and it had backfired. Yes, he was willing to claim responsibility for the plan going awry, but he also felt guilty—an emotion he hadn't been plagued with ever since he could remember.

But the fact remained. Wynter had been attacked on his watch. She'd been hurt and would bear the bruises and marks of it for weeks to come, and Marcus wished he could take them away. Not only for her benefit, but also his own. He didn't want to have to see them and be reminded of how he had failed her.

"Thank you," he told his witch, and the Priestess said nothing in response. She knew what the appreciation was for. She had saved Wynter while he was off playing his power games with Warren. Teaching him a lesson he'd thought was entirely justified at the time, when he ought to have been taking care of the woman he had insisted stay there with him. The woman he cared for, whether he was willing to admit it or not.

"I have the perfect protector in mind for her, my lord," the Priestess said, as though having read his mind about Wynter needing an official guard. Once again, they were on the same page.

"Don't say a shifter," he groaned, "we all know how frustrating they can be. And disloyal." The Priestess laughed and shook her still cloaked head.

"No, my lord. I was thinking of a jinni. A powerful and loyal presence that can watch over her day and night, but someone Wynter wouldn't even realise was there. And it just so happens I know where we can find one."

A grin spread across Marcus's face and he nodded to his impressive witch. With just that one suggestion she had outdone herself, and won back his favour. Jinn were notoriously reclusive and hard to command, but once someone was taken on as their charge, they were theirs and would protect their host until that person died, but then they were rewarded by being turned into one of their kind. It was either that, or the host was transformed into a vampire first, just like the Priestess had told him Wynter would be.

Their path, it seemed, was on course to that outcome like foretold. Marcus still didn't feel comfortable merging, but that aversion was already waning somewhat. As if it were being replaced with another fear. The fear of losing her, or of someone defiling the perfect creature he so enjoyed moulding and grooming to be his flawless companion.

Whichever way it worked out, Marcus was beginning to accept that she was soon going to have to turn away from her human heritage and become one of the immortal elite. And it was worth it knowing she would be safe from any other harm and securely by his side once she transitioned.

Damn, was this actually going to happen? It sure seemed so.

The Priestess had been given the go ahead, and would undoubtedly have the jinni under her wing by dawn. She would see to it that he or she was delivered to the club without delay, and Wynter's protection would be in place before her next shift was even over.

The deed would be done without his darling young

woman ever even knowing it, and she would be under the ruthless creature's magical protection from that moment onwards. And there would be no mercy for any creature who tried to come between a jinni and their charge. David's fate was nothing to that of an execution by Jinn. They were renowned for their dark forms of justice, and an even darker sense of humour. They often decapitated their oppressors and stripped the flesh from their bones before mounting them on their walls like some kind of macabre décor.

One notorious feud had ended with an entire household of vampires being strung up and drained of blood before being left to rot within a magical cage no one but the jinni could enter. After a decade of starvation the patient captor had then relieved them of their skins and had them made into a leather chair, but yet he'd still refused to kill them. To this day, not a soul knew the rest of what'd happened to the family of vampires, but the story was an infamous lesson to any and all who dared make an enemy of a jinni.

This was going to be perfect.

FOUR

Wynter woke later that afternoon and, for a glorious moment, she forgot all about what had happened with David earlier that day. For just a few seconds, all was well, but then she shuffled on her pillow and felt the knees beneath it, reminding her of how she'd fallen asleep in the Priestess's lap. And of course, she then remembered exactly why the strange witch had watched over her in the first place.

She turned her head to look up, expecting to see the same shrouded woman as before, but it wasn't her. It was Marcus. He seemed thoughtful and was looking off in the distance, as if he hadn't realised she'd awoken.

"Hey," she croaked as she rubbed her eyes and sat up. She figured the best thing was actually to compose herself and keep her distance, so she went to move down towards the opposite end of the sofa, but Marcus evidently had other ideas. He reached out and grabbed her before she could move away and then pulled her to him and held her close, his intense blue eyes swallowing her whole.

"Good afternoon, Wynter," he said with a smile, "I've enjoyed watching you sleep. It was very…

peaceful."

Wynter's first instinct was to joke with him about being creepy, but she didn't. She just smiled and thanked him. It was actually nice to know she hadn't been left alone, even while she was out of it. Marcus and his Priestess had cared for her when she'd needed them most, and Wynter knew she wouldn't forget it in a hurry.

His breath then suddenly hitched and Wynter peered back into his eyes. She figured he wasn't used to having someone be genuinely happy to see him, and she shook her head.

"All these people who love you, and yet you're surprised when I offer you some real warmth?" she asked timidly.

"I understand how my curse works. I also accept their affection because I know it isn't real. But with you, everything *is* real. Often overwhelmingly so," he groaned, but thankfully didn't push her away. Wynter still needed the closeness. In fact, she wanted even more. Her body ached all over from David's rough treatment, and she knew sex ought to be the last thing on her mind, yet she wanted Marcus to touch her. To make her feel good again and, albeit rather strangely, as though she was still desirable and untainted in his eyes.

She placed a gentle kiss against his lips and arched her body against his, and Marcus reacted exactly the way she had hoped. He held her tighter and kissed her back, soft at first and then harder. His lips were so forceful they bruised hers. His hands pressed into her hips so hard she knew he'd leave marks. But she didn't care. Unlike David's bruises, she welcomed them, along with the silent promises she could feel his body making hers.

Damn, this was so confusing.

When she eventually pulled away and sucked deep lungful's of air into her chest, it was no surprise to see Marcus's eyes shining brightly from somewhere deep within him. They were the most beautiful things she had ever seen and Wynter knew she ought not to be drawn to that shining beacon calling to her from inside of him, but couldn't help herself. She was meant to be following him to that woman in her apparition, not letting her soul merge with his. She was meant to be keeping a safe distance. And yet, all she wanted in that moment was for him to love her. To share his life with her, and his soul.

"Tell me what you want, Marcus," she croaked, "tell me what you need."

"I want you," he answered her, and pulled her closer still, "I need you."

Wynter thought about ripping off her clothes and throwing herself at his mercy. She had stayed away from having any real sex all week, but now all she could think about was having him inside of her. She yearned for it like an addict, but something still told her it was no use. He wasn't going to give her it, no matter what he truly wanted.

And he'd called her the fighter in their little tête-à-tête.

Before he even said another word, the shutters went down. Marcus retreated back into his usual cold shell and Wynter shuddered against the sudden chill that swept over the room.

She didn't need telling no. In fact, she didn't want to hear it at all, and so she climbed up out of Marcus's lap and walked over to the bathroom without another word.

Inside, she threw her pyjamas in the wash basket and climbed straight into the shower. Wynter turned up the heat and got to work on her wash routine, all the while telling herself it was better this way. She would remain free as long as he kept her at arms length and that was still the ultimate goal. To keep hold of the freedom she had fought so hard to get back until she could get away from him completely.

After rinsing the last of the conditioner from her hair, Wynter finally opened her eyes and looked down at herself. It took a minute for her to take in the damage and attempt to get her head around what she was seeing. The bruises had now had time to develop. Her wrists were littered with cuts and were both purple where David had held them while he'd forced his kisses on her. Her legs had huge bruises on them too from where he'd thrown her down on the ground and wrenched them apart, and Wynter screwed her eyes shut, trying to force away the memory of her kicking and fighting him as he held her down and tried to force himself on her.

But it was no use. The memory was too fresh. The feeling of his hands roughing her up too real. Her pain too present. It was all just far too powerful to overcome.

Her knees hit the shower floor first, and Wynter let herself tumble down onto the ground without a care for the extra bruises it might cause. She felt lost and afraid all over again, and let her tears flow. The world was suddenly no longer full of any hope or wonder like before, but an awful place and she knew there was no good left. There was nothing left to fight for.

She'd clung to her strength for so long, but the Priestess was right.

It was all a lie.

She wasn't strong.

Nothing was right.

She was alone and unloved.

Wynter didn't move. She just sat there and continued to cry her heart out, even when she was enveloped from behind and pulled into the strong arms of the vampire she knew would always hold her, even if he couldn't bring himself to properly love her.

Marcus was still fully clothed and his wet shirt clung to his chest as Wynter nestled herself against him, turning see-through. She started unbuttoning it, but he shook his head no. "I want you, Wynter, but not like this," he whispered, "I told you before, you're here to feed me. The rest is none of my business."

She saw red.

Wynter pushed herself out of his hold and clambered to her feet. She didn't care that she was naked, all she wanted was to get away. On wobbling legs, she grabbed a towel and then ran for the door, leaving Marcus still sitting beneath the cascading water.

She made it to the lift and threw herself inside the second it opened, and thought for a moment she was going to get away unscathed, but then Marcus appeared and shoved his hand between the doors and forced them back open. He was dripping wet but didn't seem to care. Like her, he was clearly fraught and his emotions were all over the place. Wynter could read him that well at least.

He looked a wreck, but he was also raging, and she pressed herself against the back wall of the elevator in absolute fear.

"I never thought I'd say this, but you win, Marcus," she then sighed dejectedly, "I'll never ask you for anything ever again. You can feed and then I'll leave to recuperate alone rather than let myself get even more confused by your mixed signals. These emotions within me aren't real, or at least you keep telling me so, and I'm finally learning not to trust my heart, but my head. I can't stand it any longer. I can't want you when all you want me for is my blood."

Wynter then looked up over his shoulder and saw the clock on the wall turn to six-pm. Her overtime shift was done. Their time was up. He knew it too and took a step back so that the lift doors could close at last, his eyes on hers the entire time, yet he didn't say a word. Marcus didn't even try to fight her on any of it, and she was left wondering if he'd ever actually cared at all.

***

The second Wynter was gone, Marcus unleashed his

rage upon everything within his reach. He told himself it was for the better, but the pain and anguish resonating through him said otherwise. Why couldn't he just accept her? What was wrong with him to make him force her away like he repeatedly did? There were others who readily accepted love into their lives, but he just couldn't bring himself to say yes to her when she begged for him to love her. There was no reason why he shouldn't take her, and yet he'd let her go thinking he didn't care again, just like all the other times.

He couldn't fathom why he was so averse to letting their souls merge, but figured it was a power thing. To give part of himself over was a fate worse than death for a control freak such as he. And so, once again, he had pushed Wynter away. Told her no. Let her believe he didn't care for her. All he'd done was watch as she disappeared out of sight, rather than stop her. Rather than tell her he did care and wanted to love her, but was scared.

And there it was. The true reason—he was scared.

That realisation only angered him further and Marcus picked up the nearest thing to him, a lamp, and hurtled it towards the glass wall that had until that second served as a partition to his top floor office. It shattered with ease and Marcus didn't stop there.

He trashed the entire room. Ripped apart the sofa that still smelled of Wynter. Emptied the drawers of her new clothes and shredded them. Broke apart his huge wooden desk where she had perched naked before him and shattered it into a thousand pieces.

So, this was what it felt like to win?

He couldn't think of anything worse.

FIVE

Wynter had never been so grateful for her stash of essential supplies before in her entire life. She had the spare clothes hanging in her office closet, and had even brought underwear and shoes in on the off chance she might need them. And now she needed them desperately. There was no hairdryer so she had to leave her dark hair to dry in waves, but it wasn't the end of the world and she made a mental note to bring in a spare for next time. Everything else was readily to hand in her gloriously private office and it wasn't long before she was dressed up, made up, and ready to start her usual night's work.

All was well, on the outside at least. Underneath the façade, she was a right royal fucking mess. What the hell else was new? She contemplated, but then forced all of her emotions, anxieties and pain away. She went back to adopting her utter coldness and fired up her computer before then busying herself with the usual admin of answering emails and moderating the website boards while updating each of their private sites.

Immersing herself in work was bliss. It worked a treat to distract her from the wreck of a life she had created for herself. After all, who needed therapy when you had procrastination and denial?

Hunger pains were soon niggling in her gut though and after a couple of hours' spent working solidly, she gave into them and poked her head out of her office door, checking to see whether the coast was clear.

There were workmen outside in the hallway though. They were heading up and down in the lift to Marcus's office and Wynter frowned. What on Earth were they up to?

She stepped out, locking the door behind her, and then approached one of the men.

"Hey, what's going on upstairs?" she asked with a gentle smile.

"Mr Cole has asked us to redecorate his office," he answered, and was about to head back into the lift when Wynter put her hand on his arm.

"I have some things up there. Would it be okay if I came up and grabbed them?" she asked, thinking of her clothes and her handbag that was still in Marcus's office from when she'd been down to get them that morning before running into David—someone she didn't want to be thinking about right now though so forced that thought away.

"No, Miss. The room has been cleared already and everything has been binned. It's now't but an empty shell," he replied, and then left in the awaiting elevator.

Wynter stormed over to the desk where Bryn was sat typing at his computer, and he turned to her with a smile, which dropped when he saw how enraged she was.

"Miss Armstrong, what's wrong?" he asked, his tone gentle in a practised bid to diffuse the tension.

"What's Marcus playing at?" she demanded, and then lowered her voice. "My handbag was upstairs. Please tell me it's not been thrown out in all the rubbish?"

Bryn looked sheepish. He checked down the corridor to ensure they weren't going to be overheard, and then leaned closer to her with a frown.

"If it was up there, then it left in pieces," he told her, "this was not a planned redecoration, put it that way. It sounded like an animal had gotten loose in there." Bryn then looked her up and down, one eyebrow raised in questioning.

It was obvious he thought she had something to do with whatever had gone on upstairs, and Wynter knew he was right, but she wasn't going to say so.

"He was fine when I left," she lied, "thank you anyway."

Wynter then headed for the main stairs and she bounded down them to the basement. She told herself that she wasn't looking for a certain someone, but for the group of people she felt safe amongst. The team she was part of, despite what she had told Warren the last time she'd seen him. She just needed somewhere safe to hide out until she could figure out what was going on with Marcus, but as she stalked down a bunch of questions were whirring around in her head.

Had he trashed the office because of what had been said and done between them? Was his refusal of her all lies and bravado? Did he truly care?

His soul had been shining out at her from behind those pale blue eyes numerous times, and Wynter knew that reaction had been real. It wasn't a lie or something she'd imagined thanks to her raging hormones, but Marcus had still pushed her away, in spite of it all. He had let her go, rather than beg her to stay, and so he was to blame for however he'd felt in the aftermath of their fight. If he was angry enough to lay waste to his own office, then it was on him. She'd tried and tried to get him to stop hiding, so wouldn't let herself feel guilty about how he chose to unleash those emotions when her back was turned.

Inside the open-plan IT office, Wynter went straight for the kitchenette and she poured herself a large coffee before grabbing one of the bagels from the cupboard and popping it in the toaster.

She then spied Phoebe across the room and offered her a wave, and was pleased to see a welcoming smile on her face as she dropped what she was doing and came bounding over.

"Hey, where have you been?" Phoebe asked when she reached her, "we've missed you." Wynter gave her an awkward smile. She'd stayed away on purpose after her fight with Warren. She'd told him she wasn't one of them and didn't want to be, but it was all lies. Pain she had to put upon him to help her force him aside. It was nice to know he hadn't relayed her hurtful words to the rest of the team though.

"Missed you too, Phoebe," she replied, and then gave her a small hug. "Things have been mental upstairs. Plus I had a run in with Warren yesterday," she added, thinking a bit of honesty wouldn't hurt.

"Ah, so that's why he's been such a delight," Phoebe replied with a knowing smile. "I know he hates Fridays and Saturdays because of the obvious, but he's not usually such a miserable arse as he has been this weekend. I thought it must've been because he took a bigger beating both days than usual."

Wynter frowned. Warren was hurt?

She looked around for him, but he wasn't there. He wasn't even in his makeshift office behind the frosted glass partition. Surely he wasn't home sick?

"Is he okay?" she asked, and Phoebe shrugged. "Where is he?"

"He's still in one piece. We all have good weeks and bad. He'll get over it," she replied sullenly, "and he's up in marketing helping Marcella with something. He'll be back in a few minutes."

Wynter sighed in relief. She couldn't have handled

it if Warren was in too bad of a state. Not after she'd seen for herself just how nasty it was in that ring.

They sat down and she started eating her bagel with a frown. She tried to pretend she didn't care, but truly did. She wanted to see if he really was okay, or if Marcus had somehow hurt him some more. She didn't trust that he would've left Warren alone while her back was turned.

She'd seen Marcus lash out at him on Friday morning after Warren had rejected her, but other than his fighting in the ring, as far as Wynter knew they hadn't had any altercations. Unless perhaps Marcus had given him more vampires to spar with over the Saturday daytime? Had he given him a heavy workload in the knowledge that he wouldn't be able to cope, just to spite him, and also Wynter? Had he done his best to make sure Warren was beaten and broken so that she no longer desired him so?

Wynter didn't doubt he would be capable of such things, and felt her despair surge within, as if it were a growing, living thing.

"And he's miserable? Or just in pain?" Wynter asked, and she couldn't deny the ache she felt in her chest when Phoebe reached across and put her hand over hers. It was such a gentle, tender thing to do, and still the gesture spoke volumes. Kindness. It cost nothing, and yet Wynter felt it was just another debt she owed. Another person she would have to fret over.

"Both," Phoebe answered, "and something tells me you're exactly the same."

Wynter burst into tears and didn't even try to quieten them when half the room turned to stare at her in shock. She even let Phoebe gather her in her arms and hold her. It was wonderful, but still her tears kept flowing, no matter how many minutes ticked by.

Her week had been hell. Wynter had hated her new life one day, loved it the next, and then feared it just enough to earn back some semblance of her freedom by the end. She was glad of her new job, yet her heart was now full of nothing but contempt for the vampire who had given her it.

"What the fuck?" Warren's voice permeated the chaos, but Wynter ignored him. She kept her face buried against Phoebe's shoulder and clung to her tighter.

"Back off," Phoebe replied, and Wynter heard Warren mutter beneath his breath, but he did as she had asked. He stayed away.

The sound of a spoon hitting the inside of a mug then reached her, as did the smell of fresh coffee. Next, she heard a chair being pulled out near to her and someone took a seat with a thud.

Gulp. Gulp.

Did he have to drink it so loud?

Gulp.

It took Wynter a few moments to realise she was no longer crying. To notice how she was listening for him, rather than pouring her anguish out onto poor Phoebe's blouse. She shuffled a little and turned her head just enough so that she could see him out the corner of her eye.

Warren was sitting two chairs away, his back straight and his arms out in front of him on the table, a mug still cradled in his hands. He had cuts and bruises all over his face and neck, as well as on his knuckles and wrists.

Wynter could also see the feeding marks. So many littered his skin, not hidden even by the tattoos etched upon every inch of his flesh. And there were too many. It wasn't fair.

"Is that my fault?" she croaked.

Warren didn't even look at her. He just stood and stormed back over to where the pot of coffee was sat waiting.

"You guys want one?" he asked.

"Yeah," said Phoebe.

"Yeah," echoed Wynter.

He delivered them without any care for whatever sloshed over the side, and Wynter had to laugh. Warren certainly wasn't the delicate sort, so she wasn't surprised in the least. In fact, she smiled to herself in spite of the ache still radiating in her chest.

The three of them sat in silence for a while, and Wynter eventually peeled herself from Phoebe so she could pluck up her coffee and take a sip. It was perfect, and made just as she liked it. Fresh tears threatened, but she beat them back and took a deep breath before finally looking up and over at Warren. He was sitting waiting patiently and she appreciated him giving her the time to gather herself. He hadn't pounced, and he hadn't come in shouting or screaming either. He'd simply let her be.

"None of this is your fault, Wynter," he groaned, and then sighed, "don't ever think that." She didn't believe him. "Those bloodsuckers did this. Not you."

The air between them then suddenly heated and Wynter glared at Warren.

"Don't be so naïve," she demanded with a frown, "he knows I—" she hesitated, but knew she had to be honest. She had to tell him.

Phoebe seemed to sense that things were about to head towards the deep and meaningful, so she pushed back in her chair and deposited her mug beside the sink. She hovered there a moment, waiting for Wynter to give her the go-ahead to leave, which she did.

A second later, she and Warren were alone. He moved into the empty chair between them and took her hand in his, peering into her eyes intently.

"He knows what?" he asked her, "that I care for you? That I want you? He does know. Mr Cole told me himself."

"He did?" she cried, and Warren nodded. She softened and leaned into him ever so slightly, craving his warmth and comfort. "Well, I was going to say that he knows I care for you, Warren. He isn't jealous with any of the managers, and yet with me it feels different. He added the extra day for me to feed him, but there's more. He touches me. Acts like he wants me in ways I'm not sure I can handle."

"It's all part of his games, Wynter. He plays them with all of us, but just stay strong and be his slave when he needs you to be, and then be yourself in between. The curse can only invade us so much," Warren replied, and Wynter cringed. She was free of at least that one element, and being close to Warren now, she knew it was worth giving up that freedom for. He was alive, albeit a little battered, and it was all because of her sacrifice.

Totally worth it.

"I think I can manage that," she replied as she turned her face up to look into his. Warren was rugged and hardened. His features weren't soft, even hidden behind his beard and the dark eyes that now burned into hers. He had seen his share of evil and yet had remained a good and honest soul. And one she wanted to know. Perhaps, even wanted to fall for.

Before she could say another word, his lips were on hers.

Warren's kiss was as wild as he was and his beard scratched at her face, but Wynter loved it. She put her hand on his cheek and kissed him back, and it wasn't long before their kiss turned feverish and full of longing.

She wanted him and knew now how he wanted her just as much. There was no question of their attraction to one another, and when he eventually pulled away, Wynter felt lost without him. This was dangerous, they both knew it, but she didn't care.

SIX

Warren stood and pulled Wynter to her feet with a grin. She quickly followed his lead and soon they were heading away from the kitchenette and over towards the back of the room where the pillars of servers were located, and she saw how their kiss hadn't gone unnoticed by the other members of the IT team. Eyes were on them and followed the pair as they passed, as well as the smiles and nods of approval. It was good to know their team approved of what had just sparked to life so publicly between them.

"This is where we come to rest or to get some peace," Warren told her when he eventually came to a stop, and he turned the handle on the door to what Wynter had assumed was a broom closet or an electrical cupboard. Inside, she found a small space that had been cleared of janitorial goods and they'd been replaced with cushions, blankets and even a massive beanbag that she figured she might actually be able to fit her entire body on.

She let out a giggle and kicked off her shoes before clambering straight onto the beanbag, and then held up her hand to let Warren know how she wanted him there with her. He took it and obliged her, taking up the entire leftover space with his huge body when he joined her on the small makeshift bed.

"Hold me," Wynter whimpered, shuffling closer, and Warren did as she asked. He wrapped her in his arms and pulled her close. Their bodies were soon pressed tightly against each other's, and while Wynter wanted more, she didn't push for it. Fear held her back. Terror over what Marcus would do if he caught them. If he figured them out.

Warren let his hands roam over her back and up to her face though, where he cradled it and pressed his lips against hers once again.

His next kiss was ferocious and somehow gentle at the same time. His lips caressed her mouth, his tongue delving inside and taking charge of her senses, and Wynter swooned. She hadn't felt like this since when she and her ex were first seeing each other. In fact, even before then. Back to when her heart had still been full and she had been ready to love. Open to anything. The endless possibilities and a determination to prove her mother's cynicism about men wrong.

And yet, Wynter knew it was her who had been wrong. Her heart had believed in something that hadn't existed, or at least that was what she'd come to believe after nothing but heartbreak after heartbreak.

She bristled and pulled away, and Warren looked at her with a sorrowful expression. Did he feel it too? She thought he must do. Did he know their best-laid plans were fruitless in the face of the powerful and predatory boss they were both fighting against in their own way?

"This isn't over. He hasn't won," he groaned, confirming her suspicions, "we'll find a way to be together."

"He'll kill you if he discovers we're fooling around behind his back, Warren," Wynter croaked. She knew Marcus would do it, but she also knew something her beau did not. She was only still under his employ because of her deal with the vampire tyrant to keep Warren alive. If he went back on their deal, then she'd be gone, and Wynter hoped that'd be enough to ensure he never lashed out at him to spite her.

Marcus would always be selfish. Always put himself and his needs first, even if that meant having to keep Warren around, and that gave her a certain amount of control. It was only a little, but it was still something.

"Then we shall lie," he answered with a smile, "we'll still know the truth, but when he's around we'll both hide how we feel. Keep it secret."

"Even if we have to keep our distance and hide our feelings, we'll know the truth," she agreed. "But what if he kisses me, or touches my body in the throes of the feed?"

"Then you close your eyes and think of me, Wynter," he groaned, and she felt heat rage from inside of her at the thought. "Imagine it's my hands on you. My lips," Warren continued, and she arched herself against him, desperate to feel his body crushing hers.

One day, she told herself. When Marcus was over his infatuation with her and he'd calmed down with his mind games. When she was free to live and work in peace through the week, and then feed without all the chaos at a weekend. That was when she and Warren could be together for real. When she could spend the day making love with him and being a normal couple. They might even fall in love and live happily ever after.

Maybe...

Thud, thud, thud!

"Guys, you need to wrap up whatever you're doing in there and get out here quick!" Phoebe's voice permeated their little bubble, and Warren jumped to his feet in record speed. He opened the door and reached down for Wynter, who was just climbing up onto her shaky legs. She felt exhausted and in need of some sleep, but the look on Phoebe's face told her they weren't going to be allowed any more quiet time. Her eyes were wide and she seemed terrified, as if she had seen a ghost.

"What is it?" Warren asked her.

"It's David... he's dead," she replied, her voice shaking.

"Oh, God," Wynter croaked, holding her stomach that'd just begun to ache at the news finally being out amongst the others at the club.

"Mr Cole called directly to inform me and to say he's going to come down and see me. There was some kind of accident and he fell down three flights of stairs," Phoebe explained, and then her knees buckled and Warren caught her in his arms, holding her close.

Wynter was frozen solid. She didn't know what to say or do, and wasn't sure why Marcus had told Phoebe the news, or why he'd lied. There had to be a reason. She got her answer when Warren eventually turned to her with a grim expression on his dark face.

"Her cousin," he whispered, and she nodded.

"I know he had his moments, but he was a nice guy. Wouldn't hurt a fly," Phoebe said, still looking shocked, as if she couldn't get her head around the sombre news. "Oh my poor Aunt Nancy."

"When did it happen?" Warren asked.

"Sometime this afternoon while everyone was either out or working their overtime hours," she replied, and began to sob. "He was just found by some contractors because they were using the service entrance rather than the usual one. Everyone just thought he was off doing his checks."

Wynter couldn't listen to any more. She put her hand on Phoebe's arm in a bid to be supportive but all she wanted to do was escape. She couldn't bear to hear how he was such a great guy, when he was dead only because he'd tried to attack her. Marcus could play it off as an accident all he wanted, but she would always know the truth.

"I have to go," she groaned, before adding a robotic, "I'm sorry for your loss."

Warren opened his mouth as if to stop her, but Wynter just walked away. She couldn't stay and listen to this fabricated story any longer. She felt bad for what'd become of poor David, but at the same time she was also angry. She had been attacked and no one would ever know it. They'd never learn just how horrible David had been or how much he'd hurt her.

She reached the huge open-plan office and ignored the quizzical looks from the engineers as she passed through the small group and headed straight for the door. The last thing she wanted to do was explain what'd happened between her and Warren, or discuss what Phoebe had gone running to tell them both. Wynter just wanted to hide herself away again.

She flung open the door just as Marcus was coming through it and full on collided with him. He was like a wall against her flimsy human body and she crashed into him and stumbled backwards.

He reached his hand out and caught her around her lower back, the move serving to not only stop her from tumbling to the ground, but also yanking her flush against him.

"Tread carefully, Miss Armstrong," he whispered in her ear as he held her there, and she couldn't ignore the menacing tone to his voice.

"Or what?" she challenged, but Marcus ignored her. He let go and moved past her in a swift and fluid movement, holding the door open so that Wynter could escape like she'd planned.

She wanted to refuse him and stay, but knew she had no other choice than to leave them to it. He knew she was flummoxed, of course, and Marcus simply shut the door in her face with a sly smile, while all she could do was walk away with a huff.

***

Marcus was being petty, he knew it, but couldn't help himself. The look on her face as Wynter had collided with him had been thoroughly amusing. Her reaction to him shutting the door in her then shocked face, however, had been priceless.

She'd been trying to hide from him ever since their fight, but he wasn't really the kind to dwell. Yes, he'd lashed out in the moment, but his rage had quickly subsided. After he'd trashed the office it had just been a few minutes before he was setting in motion a plan to have it back up and running again before the night's end.

The redecorated office would have everything he needed in it and then some, including a properly sectioned off area for Wynter to call home. A place where she could be locked away and stay safe from any and all others during the daytime.

The space was not for the additional managers, of course, but only her. He had offloaded his anger after she'd run from him and had now seen sense. He did want her, he couldn't fully deny it, and so had perfected a different kind of plan to make her stay with him.

Marcus wasn't going to let her leave, not even on the days she wasn't obliged to stay and feed him. She would fight his decision, sure, but he was ready for her this time, and of course he had three thousand years worth of strategies at his disposal. She was no match for him and his superior strengths of both prowess and will. The sooner she accepted it the better.

Wynter had of course admitted defeat, but that wasn't good enough. Marcus wanted her broken and completely at his disposal. He'd had enough of her evasion tactics, and even more so of her strong and independent woman routine.

She might not say so out loud, but she wanted someone to love her, and Marcus wanted to ensure she never found it. He was also going to make damn sure she never tried to get close enough to ask him again. The comfort and warmth had to go. He was determined not to give her anything else other than his usual attention while administering his bite. Wynter was his slave, not his lover, and it was time she learned that.

And yet, he couldn't force aside the memory of her body as it'd called to his. Not only with her words, but also with her soul. She had wanted him to make love to her, and not for the first time. Was her soul really his for the taking? No, he reminded himself. She was only there because he had forced her to be. Plus there was that little show with Warren at that table. And then they'd disappeared into the back together? Nope. Not on his time, or under his nose. The boy had been threatened before about touching what wasn't his, and Marcus wasn't against issuing him with a polite reminder.

He carried on inside the huge department and then sat with Phoebe and fed her his lies while also using his power over her to ensure she believed everything he said. She was smitten with him in no time and had soon forgotten any questions she might've had about her cousin's untimely demise. She believed it to be an accident. Plain and simple. Case closed.

That task over with, Marcus then turned his attention to Warren. He had spent the afternoon beating the little rabbit to within an inch of his life and then watching as his clients fed from him, and had thoroughly enjoyed himself. Enough that he wanted to toy with him some more. To savour the flavour of the boy's defeat.

"What fun we've had today, you and I," he told Warren as he entered his small section of private office and closed the door behind him.

Marcus watched as he fought with his conscience

about whether to answer him back. Anger flared within him and yet Warren remained calm and collected. He couldn't deny that he was impressed. "But it seems you need reminding of a few things, little rabbit…"

"I haven't touched her," Warren barked, still fighting his urge to properly argue back. "I promise. Wynter came to talk with me and we did, that's all."

"All of it?" Marcus replied knowingly and he watched with a satisfied smile as Warren squirmed under his scrutiny. He then took a seat opposite him at the small desk and grinned from ear to ear. "Shall I tell you what happened after I left you in that ring today? What I walked in on when I returned to my office?"

Warren squirmed and fear began oozing out of him. He was terrified of being hurt again, and given by how scared he was, it was a marvel that he was still standing.

"I'm sorry, sir. I'll keep my distance. She instigated the kiss," he eventually answered, and Marcus shook his head. Oh how easily he'd sold her out. Tried to get her in trouble rather than accept it himself.

"That's not what I was talking about."

"Then what?" Warren asked, and while he calmed a little he continued to shake with the remnants of his fear. It was utterly delightful.

"David… He loved Wynter. I knew it and she knew it. She tried to let him down gently, but then, she couldn't help herself. She loved the attention he kept on giving her and lapped it up, even when she knew it was wrong to toy with the poor boy," Marcus told him with a bogus sad look on his devious face. "When my back was turned she lured him up to my office thinking she could play with his emotions some more. She'd told him to keep their affair secret. To wait and pretend to everyone else that they were just friends, but all the while she'd promised him that when the time came they would be together. That one day they would be free to love one another openly."

Marcus watched Warren crumble from the inside out. So, he was right. She'd made similar promises to him. She'd reached out and he had believed her when she'd told him they'd find a way to be together. Warren had trusted her, but not any more. Not after what Marcus was telling him. They were utter lies, but the imbecile didn't know that, and thanks to the hex placed upon him that rendered his emotions never fully his own, he had no choice but to trust his forceful boss's word.

"No, she wouldn't. She couldn't love him," Warren croaked.

"Of course not," Marcus replied with a deep laugh, "she is incapable of love but is devious and selfish enough to pretend in order to get what she wants. Wynter likes to be adored and will do anything to have men falling at her feet. Women too."

Warren replied with a groan. He clutched at his chest and shook his head, still struggling with the news, and so Marcus pushed him harder. "David was in turmoil. She had him tied up in so many knots that when she sent him away again he couldn't stand it. He threw himself down those stairs because he could bear it no longer. It's Wynter's fault he's dead, I saw the poor boy for myself. David's death was no accident. He committed suicide thanks to what she did to him."

SEVEN

Wynter headed straight for her office and threw herself inside in an angry and petulant mood. Marcus was toying with her, Warren was right, and she hated how she was letting him. Why the hell was he being like this? She'd already admitted defeat to him once today, and she was sure as shit not going to do it again.

No sooner had she locked the door behind her that a light cackling sound from behind her made her jump. She turned on her heel and found the Priestess standing over by her window that overlooked the dance floor below. Shrouded and hidden from prying eyes, as always, she was watching the crowd. Wynter went to her, drawn to the powerful lady by not only her magnetism, but also the sense of trust that had already begun to develop between them. The Priestess had cared for her. Protected her. Kept her safe from harm when she had needed it most. The strange woman had earned a place in Wynter's good graces, and she hoped to one day call her a friend.

"My lady," Wynter greeted, using the same

term Marcus always seemed to. "To what do I owe this pleasure?"

"My love, I wished to check on you. To make sure all was well, but you are fraught. Why?" she replied, her voice still that strange sound of mixed vocals all meshed into one. It always reminded Wynter of those horror movies where the young victim gets possessed and speaks in a demonic tone. There was nothing right about the sound in the slightest, but she didn't recoil like she had the first time. She was getting used to it, and to her presence and all-seeing power, or so it seemed.

"Marcus has cruelly toyed with me," she replied honestly, "he messes with my head and my heart. I can't stand it."

"Yes," was all the powerful witch replied. The Priestess was unequivocally loyal to him, Wynter knew, but she also seemed to understand her plight. She had to know what a pain in the backside he could be, even if she wouldn't betray him by saying so. "Here, I have a gift for you," the Priestess then whispered and reached out her hand. Atop her gloved palm was a jewellery box and Wynter frowned down at it. Somehow, it felt like whatever it was inside might be about to make things worse. As if it were a dastardly trick Marcus was having the witch play on her.

"What's inside?" she asked, but the Priestess shook her head.

"You'll have to open it and see…"

"Did Marcus put you up to this?" she tried, and felt immediately relieved when the strange woman shook her shrouded head no.

"I made it for you. This token of my affection will keep you safe from harm, Wynter."

"More so than your locator spell?"

"Yes…"

She could bear the suspense no longer and opened the square box to reveal a white beaded bracelet. She reached forward and stroked the luminescent beads, and found it was made of he lightest and yet sturdiest stone she had ever felt. And the colour! It was like the fullest of moons on a clear, dark night.

It was as if the beads had been carved from some kind of marble, or glass, or… she had no idea. It truly was like nothing she'd seen before. Utterly extraordinary.

She inspected it more and found there was just one solitary black stone at the base, and as she took the bracelet and viewed it in the light, Wynter was sure she saw the blackness within the bead wisp and move, like mist. "My gift to you, my love. Wear it always and none shall be allowed to cause lasting or irreparable harm to you. Not even your master."

Now then, why hadn't she led with that? Such a gift would be perfect, as long as it were true.

Wynter did as she'd commanded and slipped her hand through the circle of beads, and felt a strange shudder pass over her when they clasped tightly around her wrist. She figured the bracelet had to have been empowered with some kind of protection spell and, while it was strange to be so used to such things nowadays, she thanked the Priestess.

She then watched the shrouded woman for a moment before looking down on the throbbing sea of partygoers below them. She'd forgotten it was Saturday night and felt a pang of longing as she watched the humans dancing and enjoying themselves at the club. So unaware of whose establishment they were in. So innocent of the danger all around.

Wynter envied them.

"I guess I'd better get some work done," she told the Priestess, eyeing the clock. It was one-am.

"But you don't want to, do you?" she replied knowingly, "you still want to rebel against him. To be disobedient and have a little fun."

"Yes, but I know he won't allow it," Wynter replied dejectedly.

"What he doesn't know won't hurt him..." the Priestess told her, and she could hear that she was smiling thanks to her jovial tone.

Someone then knocked on her office door, and Wynter watched as the witch disappeared from sight in the blink of an eye, rather than be present when she opened it. She almost didn't, but was glad she'd decided to because on the other side of her office door stood Marcella. She was grinning mischievously and came bounding inside without having to ask for an invitation.

"Hey, what's up?" Wynter asked, but Marcella just eyed her up and down, her finger tapping her chin thoughtfully.

"Lose the blazer and unbutton your blouse a little," she ordered, and Wynter did as she asked, her brow furrowed in questioning. "Great, much better. Come on," Marcella then commanded, taking her by the hand.

"What's going on?" Wynter asked again, still confused.

"We're going to have a dance," Marcella replied, throwing in an eye roll as though it ought to have been obvious. "I've suddenly got an urge to be naughty and go enjoy myself. Don't make me go down there alone..." she added with a pout.

Wynter had to laugh. She got the feeling the Priestess was behind this but wasn't the least bit angry or upset about it. In fact, an hour of bunking off work was exactly what she could do with, and she nodded to her new friend.

"Don't have to ask me twice," she told Marcella as she followed her out into the hallway and then locked the door behind her.

The pair of them sneaked down to the dance floor, where they danced and immersed themselves deeply in the throng of people enjoying their Saturday night out in the old town. Most of the men around them were drunk and a little bit handsy, but they each just batted any wandering hands or wannabe suitors away without a care. They weren't there to pull, but to simply let off a bit of steam.

Wynter was used to the craziness a Saturday night out on the town brought with it though, and she let herself just be in the moment. She loved being back to her old self again and was under no illusion that she'd be in trouble once Marcus found out, but she didn't care. She was having fun for the first time in days and was enjoying every second of it. Plus, she had her new friend by her side and couldn't deny she was enjoying the company. The pair of them had spent those strange but hot few hours fooling around together the previous day but it didn't seem to have unhinged their friendship in the slightest. All that mattered was how they were two kindred souls who enjoyed their carefree relationship. Wynter trusted her and knew the feeling was mutual.

Once they were finished dancing, Marcella called for a break and led her to the bar, where she ordered herself a glass of water.

"And I'll have a large gin and tonic," Wynter added, and the barman gave her a nod before getting to work on her drink.

She then turned to Marcella, thinking of the conversation she had overheard between her and Marcus before she'd left them the previous day. "So, you're pregnant?"

Marcella practically spat out her drink but managed to gulp it down in time, and Wynter laughed.

"He told you?"

"Nope, I overheard you two talking," she explained and then gave her a nudge, "it's okay. Just as long as you're fine?"

"I am, thank you," Marcella replied with a soft smile, "it's only early days, but he knew, of course."

Wynter nodded. Marcus must have sensed it on her, just like he could their emotions and such. He might've known before she had.

"And you're happy?" she asked.

"Ecstatic," she answered with a beaming smile, and Wynter believed her. She was glowing, and her eyes were sparkling. Brimming with happiness. The petite redhead was lighting up the room, and in a way, Wynter envied her. Marcella must have a life outside of the club. A world of her own out there and someone who loved her. But then again, she'd said she was single, so maybe not. Maybe she was just pleased that a happy accident had come her way, and why the hell not?

The barman then brought over her drink and Wynter went to pay, but he shooed her away and walked off without a word. She shook her head. Marcus. He had to know they were there and told them to give her free drinks. How else could the guy have known? Or did he somehow just know they were fellow members of the same slave vampire team? Were the barmen and women in on the charade too? Were they all?

Wynter suddenly felt under the spotlight. One

of the bouncers was standing at the end of the bar and she caught his eye. She remembered him from her visits to the club before, but also from her nights spent there since joining the ranks of the Blood Slaves. He knew exactly who she was and Wynter realised as she took a look around at the rest of the staff members, whose eyes darted her and Marcella's way, that they probably all knew. She was no longer just a face in the crowd, but a known entity. Someone to watch and report back on. Not free in any sense of the word.

She grabbed her drink and took a long pull on the straw poking out the top. It was strong—good. Just what she needed to calm her nerves. Wynter finished the drink in record time and then she jumped down from her stool and took Marcella by the hand, indicating that she ought to go back upstairs. She pouted again but nodded. It was the right thing to do and so Wynter took the lead. All she wanted was to get out of there. Back to the quiet solace of her office.

"Thanks for that," she told Marcella when they reached the third floor and had come to a stop in the hallway. "I really enjoyed myself."

"Anytime, babe," she answered, and then the pair of them headed off in their separate directions to their offices.

By the time Wynter had unlocked the door and shuffled inside, she was feeling lightheaded. She just about managed to lock the door behind her when a wave of nausea hit and she had to quickly lie down on the small couch Marcus had thankfully placed there for her.

Her body suddenly felt heavy, and her arms and legs numb. Her eyesight even began to betray her and she forced herself to focus on the clock above her computer. There were just minutes to spare until it was two-am. Marcus would surely punish her for turning up to feed him while drunk, but Wynter knew it would be ten times worse if she arrived late or not at all.

As she tried to sit up, another thought struck her. She'd only had one drink. A double or perhaps a tad stronger, but certainly not a skin-full. Not enough to have her drunk and disorderly so fast.

Had she been poisoned? No, it couldn't be. But it was feasible that she'd been drugged. The barman. It had to be him, the bastard.

She somehow hoisted herself off the chair and to her feet, and left her shoes where she'd kicked them off on her way in. Wynter could barely stand as it was, let alone try to negotiate her way around with heels on too. They could stay behind, no big deal.

She told herself over and over to move. To work on autopilot. To just get upstairs and prove Marcus wrong. He couldn't have one of his minions drug her just so he could punish her for being late. Nope. Wasn't going to happen.

Wynter just about managed to lock her office door closed behind her and then she stumbled across the hall to the lift, having to feel the wall for the call button as her eyes were now hardly working at all.

Once inside, she pressed the number four and then slumped to her knees. By the grace of God she still hadn't passed out, but it didn't feel as if it'd be long. Sleep was calling to her and her body ached for it. But no, she had to move. Wynter told herself to just stay awake a little longer, and when the doors opened to reveal a freshly kitted out office ahead, she was forced to crawl out of the lift on her hands and knees.

"I like you this way," Marcus's voice spoke

from somewhere ahead of her, but she couldn't see him. All she could see was the ground a couple of feet away as she clambered in the direction of his voice. "On your knees and at my command."

Wynter couldn't answer. She simply slumped to the ground and then curled in on herself protectively. What was happening? She hated every second and wanted to cry.

She tried to plead with him not to punish her, but her words were nothing but garbled groans, just making Marcus laugh. She then wanted to shout at him not to be so rude, but had nothing left. No fight. No voice. Not even her last string of consciousness.

Drowsiness took her and Wynter let herself succumb to it, but somehow even when she was beneath that veil, she was still aware of herself and of her surroundings. She wasn't completely gone, but was in no way in charge of her body. It betrayed every command she gave it to move or to fight and she wanted so desperately to scream, but could do nothing even remotely close.

It was like she was trapped inside her own skin. Just another sort of prison Marcus had created for her...

***

Marcus chuckled to himself as he watched her slip under, and he leaned down, scooping Wynter into his arms like a baby. She was utterly limp and her body was splayed around him, his hold the only thing keeping her in place. He knew that should he drop her she would tumble to the ground like a broken doll, and he contemplated doing so, just to show her what he was capable of. Pain was the best form of punishment after all, but as he peered down into her face, he knew that wasn't the right approach for his little fighter. He didn't want her to be in any physical pain. Only in emotional turmoil and anguish.

That wasn't so much to ask, was it?

But for now, he would enjoy her this way. She was gone from her body and yet still lucid. Trapped inside her mind thanks to the spell Marcella had cast upon her like he had requested. Wynter was so trusting. So sweet and innocent at times. The Priestess wanted her as a friend and for her to join the pair of them as an eternal ally, he could tell, but that couldn't happen. Marcus had told her so no end of times already. But, he'd still allowed the two of them some time together to show his loyal witch that her needs had meant something to him.

First though, she had of course delivered her with the gift their new Jinn friend had provided to bind Wynter and her new protector. She'd remained shrouded and had chosen to carry on maintaining her secret identity, and Marcus knew it was partly because the Priestess enjoyed being her friend too much to reveal herself yet. She'd also played Wynter using both sides of her relevant personas and Marcus had rejoiced in her devious tactics. She'd learned from the best after all.

Wynter sighed against him and he felt her innermost desires rise to the surface. He sensed her fear, but also her longing to feel safe. To have him keep her close in her hour of need and protect her while she was vulnerable. Damn, that was new.

Marcus had never been the saviour in the story before and he wasn't sure how to deal with it.

He leaned down to place a soft kiss against her forehead and could smell the club on her. Smell the other men whose scents had marked her. Detect the tang of alcohol on her breath and in her pores. "Let's get you cleaned up," he told her, heading for the bathroom.

On the way, Marcus took a second to admire his new surroundings. Gone was the glass partition and in its place was an actual wall. He had to open a door in the centre and walk through it to get to the area on the other side, adding some privacy to the otherwise huge open space.

In there sat a new pair of sofas that were deeper set and more comfortable than his previous ones, or so his interior designer had told him. They were to become his location for feeding during the week, as well as a place for quiet contemplation should his slave of the day require it. Unlike with Wynter, he usually dismissed Jack or Joanna once he'd fed and they would sleep it off in their offices, hence the couches each of them had and the necessity for locked doors. But all of that was going to change. The dynamics of their arrangement was going to be vastly different soon and Marcus wanted to be ready for when he announced that change.

He continued on through the large space and passed the freshly remodelled kitchenette to the fully equipped bathroom still on the left side of the second room. Next to that was a new set of drawers, but only the one. And only for his things.

Wynter's clothes were now located elsewhere—in the third new room situated on the opposite side of the room where nothing but the floor-to-ceiling windows had once been. They had now been blacked out and glued shut, giving her total privacy as well as no chance of escape.

Two more new walls now blocked that same corner off and made a bedroom just big enough to house a double bed, an en-suite and a small selection of furnishings. Inside of the drawers there were simple garments for Wynter to wear for him. Not the old fashioned nightdresses he'd used to insist on, but more modern clothing. The tea dresses she liked and replacement pyjamas with warm, fluffy socks. She was going to become his captive now as well as his slave, but that didn't mean she had to wear rags or go cold.

But first, he needed her fresh and cleaned up. He wanted her body free from dirt, makeup and perfume. Just with her natural look and freshly washed scent. She was his gift to himself, after all, and he wanted her to stay perfect.

Marcus ran a warm bath and peeled away her clothes, being gentle with her in spite of his urgency. He desired her incredibly and his eyes kept going to the vein at her neck, but he forced himself to wait. To be patient.

He would have his fill in due course and the anticipation only made it better.

Wynter sighed and her eyes fluttered open when he lowered her into the deep water, but she was still completely at his command. So at his mercy that he even had to slip his arm underneath her shoulders to lift her up from behind and stop her from inhaling the fragrant water. He then washed her with his other hand and he took his time, slowly running just a simple bar of soap across her naked flesh while caressing her skin and cleaning every inch.

Her eyes followed him and Marcus knew she was slowly coming out the other side of the spell. He didn't have long before she would find some motion again. Some feeling in her hands and feet, and eventually all over. And he had a feeling she wasn't going to be happy about it.

The Priestess had warned him her listlessness would be temporary. A slow building stun that would reach a climax and then ease off again, which Marcus could tell had already begun. And so he moved slightly faster.

He finished up, pulled the plug and dried Wynter off before wrapping her in a towel and then clutching her to him again. He then carried her out to the living area but did not dwell there. Instead, he unlocked the new bedroom and took her inside.

Wynter fit perfectly in the centre of the bed. Her dark hair was back off her face and her limp, naked body looked beautifully pale in the dim light streaming in from just the open doorway.

She opened her mouth and tried to speak, her eyes wide. Her lips then pressed together and Marcus knew she was trying to say his name. "It's okay, my sweet," he told her as he climbed onto the bed alongside her. "I'm here. I won't hurt you, and I won't drink until you're better."

Her body convulsed ever so slightly and Wynter sucked in a deep breath. She then peeled back her lips and whispered three small words with as much venom as she could apparently muster.

"You. Did. This."

Marcus leaned down over her and pressed his nose to her cheek, where he inhaled the sweet, bitter taste of her rage. He willed the spell to wear off quicker. To lessen its hold over her some more so she could continue to defy him, and tried not to smile. Not to give the game away, but he couldn't do it. The ancient vampire grinned down at her and captured her chin between his thumb and forefinger.

"What are you going to do about it?" he whispered, challenging her, and then planted a deep, hard kiss against her trembling lips. He then kept his mouth against hers but let his hand rove over her body, caressing her breasts and mound while feeling as she responded at last and was finally able to start moving against him.

Wynter initially tried to pull away, but Marcus just gripped her tighter, and he pushed one knee between her thighs to pin her down. He kept on kissing her, even when she found the strength return to her hands and pushed at his chest and tried to fight herself free. Like he'd promised, he'd waited, but now that she was no longer captive in her own body, he unsheathed the razor sharp edge to his tongue and let it slice through the tip of hers.

She had fought her way out of Marcella's spell, but within a second she was under his. The power of the bite was no match for even the strongest of humans and Wynter did a complete one-eighty. Just moments before she was fighting him in a bid to get away, but now she was holding him to her and kissing him back like a woman possessed.

She gripped his thigh with her own and squeezed, and Marcus knew what she needed. What it was she was craving.

What she was always bloody craving. She certainly wasn't afraid of her sexuality.

But he wasn't going to give into her needs.

Not today.

EIGHT

Wynter was trying so hard not to let him make her feel this way, but it was no use. Marcus was in her head, in charge of her body, and invading every one of her senses thanks to his explosive kiss and his roving hands. She'd laid in that bath confused, scared, and then seething. He had done this to her, she knew it for sure now, and he'd clearly loved having her at his complete and utter mercy. It didn't matter that he'd been gentle and tentative with her bath, the fact remained that he had drugged her.

She closed her eyes and tried to think of Warren. To imagine he was the one doing this to her, and it worked for all of a few seconds until Marcus's voice was ringing in her ears, their kiss having finally broken.

"I'm waiting, little fighter. I expected more from my favourite little pet..."

Oh hell no, she thought. There was no way she was standing for being called that.

Wynter knew it might be exactly what Marcus expected of her, but she did as he asked and fought back. She pushed him away and clambered from the bed, charging for the door regardless of her nakedness. There would be clothes somewhere for her to grab, surely. Or at least a towel or a new throw from on the sofa outside.

She reached the door and put her hand down in search of the handle, but there wasn't one there. The door was flat to the touch and no amount of pushing on it or searching for a handle made the damn thing budge.

The sound of mirthful laughter from behind her made Wynter's blood boil. She turned on her heel and glowered at Marcus, who was lounging on the bed where she'd left him as though he didn't have a care in the world.

"That door," he then told her with that wide smile she'd come to hate, "only opens if you have the key. And I have the only one."

"You can't keep me locked in here, Marcus," Wynter demanded, "we made a deal."

"Yes I know," he replied nonchalantly, and she let out a huffed sigh. He was incorrigible!

"Marcus, will you please just speak to me?" she begged, and then she started looking around the room, checking the drawers in the hope she might find some clothes to wear so she could at least cover her modesty. Each one was empty and it wasn't long before the cold began to creep in, so it was clear she had no other choice than to climb back on the bed and under the heavy covers to get warm.

Marcus scooted aside but remained atop them, and Wynter was glad. She wanted him as far away from her as possible, even if that was just the other side of a duvet.

"What would you like to talk about, Wynter?" he then asked in a gentle, eloquent tone, "shall we discuss how you've betrayed my trust no less than three times in the past twelve hours? Perhaps you'd care to start by explaining why you left my office during the day and then invited David back up here with you?"

"What?" Wynter cried, shaking her head. That was not what'd happened and he knew it. "He followed me up here against my will and tried to force himself on me. That was not by invitation!"

"And then you sat back while my Priestess was forced to step in and take his life because of your ineptitude, before finding solace in the arms of another vampire. And, let's not forget that embarrassing moment when you dared try and seduce me again," Marcus added with a roll of his eyes.

God, she hated him. Hated all the ways he made her feel so inadequate and unlovable, and even more so because even with all of that, he still wouldn't leave her be.

"You're the worst person I've ever met. Do you know that?" Wynter croaked, but Marcus didn't seem to hear her. He clearly hadn't finished berating her and wasn't going to be interrupted until he'd completed his chiding.

"You then ran to him, Wynter. You ran to Warren and told him all about your evil master. Told him you wanted to escape me. Let him make you believe you two could become something more than what I have allowed you to be."

Marcus leaned closer and tried to cup her face with his hand, but Wynter pulled away. She didn't want him to touch her, but he gave her no choice. He reached around and grabbed her damp hair, fisting it roughly in the same palm that just a second before had been so gentle. "After all that I have done for you, how is it I'm still the monster?

"You are a monster, Marcus. You drugged me and locked me in here against my will," she seethed.

"You decided to go partying rather than do your job. That's grounds for punishment if ever there was one," he replied with a dark, knowing stare. Marcus then dipped his head and pressed his mouth to Wynter's neck over her vein.

"I won't be your prisoner. You can't do this to me," she groaned.

"When all of this is over, you won't have to be a prisoner," Marcus corrected her, "because you'll follow me anywhere. Do anything I tell you. Be anything I want you to be..." his razor-sharp tongue then cut her flesh and he began to drink.

This time, Marcus took deep gulps, rendering Wynter immobile in just a couple of mouthfuls, and she hated that he was right. She was lost to him within seconds and was indeed his. No doubt about that.

Something told her getting away wasn't going to be quite as easy as she'd once thought.

***

Marcus had his fill of Wynter's delectable blood and stopped a little too close to being dangerously short of draining her dry. Unlike the last times though, he didn't rush to tend to her or replenish her valuable blood stores with an IV bag. He simply sat back and admired the young woman who had him so smitten he wanted to scream.

The girl who made him want everything and nothing all at the same time.

Marcus knew the best thing to do would be to send her away. To be rid of her temptress ways and be free of her presence that lured him to her with every breath she took. Wynter was indeed like a drug to him. She was the perfect taste when he was in one of his sunnier moods, but also the right elixir to calm his fraught mind whenever the desire to murder or maim overwhelmed him.

The main problem, as it currently stood, was that she was the cause of a lot of such hungers. Her disobedience irked him to no end and yet he egged her on, while her coy ways enamoured him and he welcomed that sweeter side she used to toy with him.

He adored being with her, and yet she loved to defy him and rile him up. She enjoyed playing with the fire within him and Marcus knew she did it on purpose. The Priestess had led Wynter into temptation without much more than a nudge of her rebellious side and had told him so too, but he'd already known. Wynter had been nothing but trouble since the moment she'd walked into that interview room, and yet, he simply couldn't be without her.

Desire swelled within him again and he knew there was no denying it this time. He demanded satisfaction no matter how close his soul might come to merging with hers, and so he whipped back the covers and let his eyes rove over Wynter's naked flesh. She was so pale. So delicate. So beautiful.

Marcus leaned down and sucked on one nipple, relishing in both the clean taste of her skin and the natural sweetness her womanly pores seemed to ooze with.

He unbuttoned his fly and began to touch himself, just like he had when in the shower with Wynter and Marcella. He then built his climax in no time at all, thanks to the model on show for him, and before he knew it he was covering her in his release.

When it was over he sat back and let himself take a few calming breaths before deciding on what to do next. The chivalrous thing would be to clean her up and cover her over. To let her rest. But, Marcus wasn't feeling in a particularly chivalrous mood. He wanted Wynter to know she had been taught a lesson, but he also wanted her to believe she had the upper hand.

Marcus adored playing these games with her and wasn't going to put an end to them yet, so instead of cleaning her up, he leaned forward and smeared her with his release using his fingertips. He smoothed it over her skin like he was applying moisturiser, when instead it was a part of him blending with her of his accord. A part he was more than willing to share, but on his terms. Marcus even spread it over her breasts and into her belly button, and then to her thighs. Wynter's unconscious body still fought his oppression and she snapped her legs closed, much to his devious amusement.

The ancient vampire laughed to himself, thinking how even in sleep, his new favourite was getting one up on him. She was winning, even though he had taken so much from her.

Anyone else would've been nothing already. Naught but a broken shell of a person, but not Wynter. She was his little fighter and Marcus hoped she would always remain that way no matter what he put her through in the days to come.

NINE

Marcus watched Wynter on one of the numerous video cameras he'd had installed around the building. There wasn't a single place where someone could hide from him, not even in the bathrooms. After all, that was where all the good stuff happened, wasn't it? It certainly had a couple hours' earlier when Wynter had taken David up on his most generous offer of making things up to her.

It had been a pleasure to watch. A sight to behold, Wynter had sat atop that counter with her legs wide and her body on show. What wasn't to like? And of course, it wasn't like Marcus was going to do anything but continue to watch her. Yes, she was beautiful and sexy and certainly alluring, but she was also a bit awkward and she liked to joke around. He had no time for nonsense like that.

There was still nothing about that young girl which made him want her for more than her blood. But then, why was he more than ready to call David up to his office and snap his neck like a twig for going near her? It wasn't like he cared. He was a three thousand year old vampire, he didn't get jealous.

Marcus turned his attention back to the array of footage options he had in his sights and clicked on the elevator, watching as Wynter took it up to the third floor and disembarked. He checked his watch. Still five minutes to go. Five minutes and he could feed. He was more than ready. His body was aching for the nourishment she was going to bring him. He could taste her already. Smell her.

He drew a deep inhalation and realised he actually could still smell her scent from his desk. Not the subtle tones from far away, but close by. Wynter had left part of herself behind.

Marcus's senses immediately heightened and his adept nose found the source if the scent within a second. He stood and then crouched down on the floor before kneeling and pressing his nose to the ground beneath his desk. There it was. The single drop of blood that'd dripped down from her perch atop his desk. It had dried, but that didn't stop his tongue from darting out and taking back what was his.

Satisfied for now, Marcus then stood and made sure his suit and shirt were perfect. That his hair didn't have a single strand out of place. Everything had to be perfect, as usual.

And then he walked to the elevator where he stood and waited for Wynter to arrive.

***

"Shit, shit, shit," Wynter groaned as she jumped in the lift and hit the button marked with a number four. It was bang on two-am and she knew she had just one minute to get up to Marcus's office and be ready to feed him. She'd cut it close. Too damn close. It wasn't even Warren's fault either. She'd decided to check her phone and had to answer a string of messages from her friend Cossette and the time had just run away from her.

Ding! The elevator chimed, marking her arrival. Wynter checked her watch again. She still had thirty seconds and so let out a sigh. She was going to be okay.

The doors then opened to reveal her master. He wasn't sat at the desk like she'd imagined, but instead he was standing right beside the lift doors like he was either about to get in with her or he was lying in wait, ready to yank her out the second she arrived. Wynter wasn't sure which one he was going to go with, so she just stepped forward and smiled.

"Good morning, Marcus."

"Right on time, Wynter," he answered and then offered her his hand, which she took and let him lead her into the private area behind the glass partition she'd been in a few times now. It felt odd being so at ease with him, someone she barely knew and yet had already shared so much with. And yet, she clung to the hand he'd graciously let her hold, like it was the most precious thing on Earth. Marcus came to a stop beside the bathroom door. "I'd like you to take a shower."

"Sure," she answered, figuring it wasn't an unreasonable request. She'd been there almost an entire day already and was feeling a bit icky herself, so welcomed the chance to get freshened up. "Do you have products for me to use?"

"Everything you need is in the cabinet, plus I have clothing I'd like you to wear for me afterwards. Your work clothes will be washed and pressed ready for this evening," he replied with a smile that both terrified and beguiled her. She suddenly wanted to kiss him. To have his arms around her and his lips on her neck. His tongue lapping at her vein…

Wynter forced those thoughts away and knew she was only thinking them because of Marcus's power to control her and make her believe that was what she wanted, when in fact, she didn't. Not really. It took every ounce of effort she could muster, but Wynter steered herself away and instead opened the door to the bathroom.

She then walked into the huge room and was surprised when Marcus followed her in. "Undress," he commanded when she turned to look at him inquisitively.

She did as he'd asked and was even more shocked when he mirrored her actions.

As she slid off her jacket, Marcus did the same.

When she unbuttoned her blouse, he removed his shirt, and so on.

Wynter couldn't keep her eyes off him. Yes, he had that distinguished look about him on the surface, but beneath the suit was the body of a god. He was slim and perfectly toned and his skin was impossibly smooth. She desperately wanted to touch him, but kept her hands to herself, remembering her shame from before when she had dared try to seduce him. She was learning, or so she hoped, and tried not to make any more of a fool of herself.

When he was completely naked, Marcus then walked further inside the bathroom and turned on the overhead shower jets, and that was when Wynter noticed how it was a twin shower. Two heads were built into the ceiling and water cascaded down from them so that two people could shower side-by-side and still have their own space, rather than be squashed into one cubicle like she'd been used to in the past.

The two of them entered at the same time and Wynter hissed as the icy cold water hit her. She jumped out of the spray and glowered at Marcus, who was already standing under his own cold stream, seemingly without a care for the shocking temperature.

"Don't mind the cold, huh?" she groaned, whacking the heat up on her controls. Marcus peered out at her from beneath his wet lashes and grinned.

"I feel nothing, Wynter. It surprises me that you

still need reminding," he said, but she didn't believe him.

"Liar," she replied as she grabbed the shampoo and got to work on sudsing up her dark brown hair. She then rinsed and opened her eyes, going in search of the conditioner, but instead found the face of her master just inches away. She went to jump back, but Marcus grabbed her and pulled her to him, crushing her against his chest.

"I have no heart, no conscience, and no soul," he growled, "what makes you think I feel a single thing other than the desire to fulfil my need to survive?"

She still didn't believe him. Bravery reared its head inside of her again and before she could stop herself, her thoughts came tumbling out of her mouth.

"If you were a heartless monster then you'd never have created this business. You like to be entertained, Marcus. You have a need to facilitate in the survival of your own kind, but rather than create farms full of humans to expedite the blood letting, you chose to create an empire. A place for hundreds of us to come and worship you. If you felt nothing, then you wouldn't need power or your cult following of humans under your spell. You'd simply take and take and take without a care."

Marcus let out a growl and he thrust Wynter against the cool tile wall, moving her as though she weighed nothing at all. He closed the gap in a millisecond and bared his teeth when she dared smile. She knew it was stupid to antagonise him, and yet, she couldn't seem to help it. "Did I hit a nerve? One you apparently don't have?" she teased, but knew she was pushing her luck.

Wynter hadn't known what'd come over her saying those things, but something just kept on snapping within her and she couldn't help but bite back, so to speak. She knew it'd get her in trouble, but she didn't care. Just as long as it meant she'd keep some of her independence, she was willing to keep pushing him and decided she would take Marcus's punishments. Or at least she hoped she could.

He stared into her eyes as if he was looking into her soul, and Wynter was shocked to find he didn't appear to understand her at all. Marcus actually seemed lost and confused in that moment. Like he had no idea how to react. One second, he looked like he wanted to throttle her, and the next he seemed like he was about to kiss her. Maybe even more.

Their naked bodies were against each other's after all.

Strangely though, Wynter didn't feel horny for him just then. She wanted to be close to him yes, but not to make love. Not to jump his bones either. All she wanted was for him to understand and to take care of her. To accept her for what she was willing to give, but also what she wanted to keep for herself. "No more games, Marcus," she whimpered, feeling lost herself now too. "Let me feed you."

He pushed away like she'd offended him and stormed back to the other showerhead, where he ducked underneath and finished getting cleaned up without a word.

Wynter hurried through the rest of her wash routine and then followed him out of the cubicle, where they both dried up in silence and she applied some moisturiser and deodorant. She also ran a brush through her hair and left it down around her shoulders to dry.

When he was done, rather than stick around Marcus left the bathroom, stalking naked into the living area. Wynter kept her towel around herself and followed, where she found him pulling on a pair of casual black trousers and a simple blue t-shirt. It was strange seeing him dressed that way. Even after only knowing him a day, she had already become accustomed to the perfectly tailored suits and crisp cotton shirts.

"Your clothes are in there," he told her, indicating

to another set of drawers to his right. She went to them and pulled open the top drawer, where she found nothing but a single white dress. It was like a modern take on the nightgowns women used to wear in the olden days, nothing like she'd choose for herself, but she slipped it over her head without argument. The dress fell right down to her feet and swamped her, feeling less than flattering, but Wynter still didn't grumble. If this was what he'd wanted her in then so be it. She'd riled him up enough for now without also adding a further insult about his choice of clothing for her.

"Marcus," she then hummed when there was nothing but silence between them. "I'm ready."

"Sit down on the couch," he demanded and she did, thinking he'd take her wrist, but he evidently had other plans. "Open your legs and lift your skirt…"

Again, she did as he commanded. Wynter hadn't ever been one to shy away from men when it came to showing off her body, but with Marcus she felt like she was only revealing what was his. That, somehow, by covering herself she was denying him of what he rightfully owned. It felt oddly good to be naked in front of him.

Marcus climbed down and lifted her left knee up, hoicking in over his shoulder so that his face was level with her thigh. She could feel her skin prickling, ready for his bite. Her heart was racing, pounding loudly in her ears, and she began to pant. How could she want it so much? This was insane.

"Please," she whimpered, but Marcus simply placed a kiss against her skin.

"Please what?" he asked, looking up at her with a wild kind of wickedness to his stare that made Wynter tremble.

"Drink," she answered, and he seemed surprised.

"Is that all you want?" he enquired, his eyes darting to her uncovered and fully on show pussy that was mere inches from his face.

Wynter thought about it for a moment. Yes, she was horny again now. But truly, she didn't want him. She didn't even want David. All Wynter wanted was for her duty to be done so she could rest. She willed the time to pass and for Marcus to take what he wanted, and realised it wasn't for any reason other than because she was ready to get away from him. That deep down, she actually despised him for what he had forced her into.

Marcus appeared to sense the cold wave of hate that flooded through her and he grinned. "Yes. It is all you want, isn't it? To let me drink so you can be free."

Wynter simply nodded. Damn him and his tricks. "Then fight me. Tell me no. Make me force you."

"I can't," she groaned, and it wasn't for a lack of trying. Wynter's instincts were telling her to run, but the spell he'd put her under was working to override those reflexes and she could do nothing but sit there, vulnerable and at his utter mercy.

"Then I shall take my time. Make it excruciatingly slow for you until you can endure it no longer, Wynter. You think you can wind me up and there won't be consequences?" he growled, and there it was. She'd known he'd punish her somehow, and cursed herself for having been so reckless. But at the same time, she knew she'd do it again if given the chance.

"I knew there would be consequences, but I also knew they'd be worth it. I might be your slave, Marcus, but I'm not your puppet."

"We'll see about that," he replied before pressing that razor-sharp tongue of his against the artery inside her inner thigh. Marcus caught the initial gush of blood as it began to flow and then stemmed it, taking just a trickle into his mouth rather than the deep gulps like he had before. He was indeed teasing it from her, taking just a few drops at a time, and Wynter felt wonderful and horrible both at once. But then, with every drop her burdens lessened and she fell further into her ecstasy. Punishment or not, her body still roared with pleasure at his bite, and before she knew it her instincts to run and fight were quietened and all she had left was her need to serve him.

It was dawn before Marcus closed the cut to her thigh. Wynter was writhing and arching up and down on the sofa before him, her body seeking comfort in arms that simply weren't there. Release in the lover that wouldn't give her it. And when he finally closed the wound and moved away from her, she shoved the dress back down and curled into a ball on the sofa.

Reality set back in and brought with it that same sense of shame she continually fought when she was with her vampire boss. Tears sprung from her eyes and she hugged herself tighter as they began to fall. When she had finished her mini-meltdown, Wynter unfurled and pulled the throw down over herself, willing for him to just leave her alone.

Sleep took her in an instant and while she needed it, her body also continued to cry out for its gratification. Her dreams were full of dark, sensual things. Of sex and desire, and of eyes that watched her, burning her soul as her body roared with heat. She woke to find her hands between her legs. Her fingers swirling the aching bead atop her thighs. She worked it harder and harder, getting closer to her release, and then screwed her eyes shut when her orgasm took hold and she began to shudder and spasm in the wonderful rhythm her body had so desperately needed.

During her high, she saw one man's face. Warren's. She remembered his dark, brooding expression, and also the words he'd spoken that morning.

He was going to look after her. Take care of her. Make sure she wasn't manipulated or taken advantage of. He was her knight in shining armour and Wynter quickly realised how what he'd promised was the hottest thing anyone had ever offered her before. No matter how hard she'd tried not to notice him, he'd gotten under her skin, and she knew she wanted more. "Finally. I thought you'd be there forever," Marcus's voice pierced her post-orgasmic haze and she cringed at him having watched her in the throes of her self-pleasure. Wynter jumped up off the sofa and found him sitting in the chair opposite. She glared across at him, but found he didn't seem to care one little bit. He was just watching her inquisitively but then held out his hand. "Come to me," he said, but she'd already been up on her feet and was moving toward him anyway. His magnetism had drawn her closer, not his words.

She climbed into his lap and let Marcus hold her close. He pulled her against him and she inhaled his scent and moaned dreamily.

"I feel so confused," Wynter told him with a sigh, "I don't know what to think or feel."

"We all tried to warn you," he answered, as if she was just being too foolish for her own good. "You will love me, but that doesn't mean you will always like me. No one else here has ever had the guts to express it, but I understand the way the hex works." Marcus shifted her so that Wynter could look up into his face. "What you feel isn't real. How you act and what you give me is by force. But, I don't care. Trust me when I say so. All I give any kind of a shit about is fulfilling my needs and taking care of my business. The rest is just coincidental."

"I don't believe you," she countered. "I can't. If I did, I don't think I could bear being here for another second."

Marcus answered with a grin that told her he'd actually like that. To have to come and get her from her home and drag her to the club. To punish her for defying him.

"And yet, I can taste how broken you are. I can

smell the misery on you, even still. I know there's nothing out there in the real world for you, just like there's nothing out there for me either."

"And what if I chose to burn this place to the ground? Where would you turn then?" Wynter groaned, not meaning it as a threat or any kind of promise, just a last ditch effort to get her life back again, even as crappy as it might've been.

"I've always got other options, but you don't. Plus, I'd make sure you burned along with the club and all the other humans in it, Wynter," Marcus answered with a sneer.

He then plucked her hand up and pressed his lips against her wrist, where he began to drink again.

TEN

When the meeting was finally over, Wynter and the others were released and they headed for the lift as a collective. She was eager to get away but still ended up holding back so as not to overcrowd the small space, and was joined by Joanna, much to her annoyance. Wynter tried to look busy as she fussed over her notes and made a point not to look at her fellow manager, but Joanna simply couldn't seem to let her out of yet another of her jealous taunts.

"You know, he was the same with me when I first started," she told her, "couldn't get enough of me. Always keeping me back for extra overtime and giving me gifts as well as his personal time. He even took to touching me inappropriately in meetings, just like with you..."

"Let me guess, but he grew tired of you so I should expect he'll tire of me before long too?" Wynter bit back. She couldn't help herself and hated how obvious Joanna was being with her envy towards the new girl. Yes, it was clear she adored Marcus and would do anything for him. Apparently, she'd loved him and chosen to live no life outside of the club all these years even though he hadn't shown her any love in return. That was absolutely fine if it was what made her happy, but Wynter could see it hadn't. Joanna yearned for Marcus in ways she herself couldn't understand, but guessed it had to be the years of being under his spell. There was no other explanation for it. Surely no one could love such a monster without being forced to?

"He knows I'll never let him down. That I'll run toward him rather than away. With you, I can see you're resisting him. Not doing your duty. It's a wonder he's even kept you on," she retorted, eyeing Wynter as if she were just some foolish girl. If she were honest, she sometimes felt as if she was. Marcus had her head in a spin and her heart and soul in tatters. She was playing games she didn't even know how to play and always seemed to be on the losing side rather than making progress, but she wouldn't give up. Not now, not ever.

Plus there was one victory she'd had that Joanna knew nothing about. None of them did. Wynter was free. She was under no curse, just the moral obligation she had made in order to keep those she cared about safe. She could leave at any time, just so long as she was ready to face the consequences for doing so. In spite of the dark repercussions, that knowledge gave Wynter a great deal of power, and a certain authority over people like Joanna. She might be the new girl, but she was no fool. She'd beaten the system, and was the sole person able to say she'd done so.

As if to say, *I know something you don't know*, Wynter let a sly smile creep onto her face and she delighted in Joanna's surprised response. She'd clearly expected her to come back with something just as foul, but instead Wynter remained silent. Her smile screamed with everything she'd left unsaid and she could tell Joanna wasn't pleased.

She clearly wanted desperately to know what secret she hadn't been let in on. That thought made it all that much sweeter, and Wynter then happily rode down in the otherwise empty lift with her fellow manager without another word said between them.

They arrived at the third floor and Joanna got out, but Wynter remained inside. She hit the button for the basement instead and arrived in seconds. She then headed down the long hallway to the door, which buzzed open the moment she arrived.

Inside, she found Phoebe and some of the other engineers huddled around another piece of equipment like they had been the first day she'd come down. Wynter went over to them and saw that this time was different though, and there was no argument over what best to do with an old piece of kit, just silence.

The group of them were standing around a laptop, which was open and had a webpage up, and they were each reading it.

Wynter moved closer and tried to see what it was, but couldn't make it out.

"What's going on?" she asked the man to her right. Palmer, she seemed to remember his name was.

"Mr Cole has split our team up. Half are heading to the new club after tonight and the rest will stay here. Bryn has just sent us a group email with the list," he answered with a frown.

Wynter was about to ask what would be so bad about that, but deep down, she already knew. These people had stuck together for years. Looked out for each other and seen to it that they were treated as family. None of them wanted that to be torn apart.

Her heart then lurched as another thought struck her. Was Warren moving to the new site too? If so, she'd hardly get to see him, and Wynter knew that would be exactly what Marcus would want. Maybe that was why he was so standoffish in the meeting? Why he was being so cold?

"That's terrible. Why doesn't he just hire new IT staff?"

she asked, but then shook her head. She already knew the answer. Marcus had trust issues. He would never employ a wholly new team and she knew it. "So, who's going?"

Palmer reeled off a few names and Wynter looked around at the relevant peoples' sour faces. They weren't happy, which was understandable.

"Plus me and Phoebe," he then told her, and Wynter's stomach dropped. As much as she hadn't wanted to hear Warren's name on the list, the idea of losing Phoebe was also a huge blow, and she looked over at her with a sad smile. Phoebe returned the gesture and then worked her way over to Wynter so they could talk.

"When Mr Cole came down to talk to me about David's death, he also told me about the move. I was sworn to secrecy until it became official, but I've been promoted to the Head of IT for the new club. We'll only need a small team there and I'll report directly to Warren so will be here for meetings and stuff," she then told her, and while happy to hear about the promotion and how she'd continue to see her new friend, Wynter was still sad about the news overall.

"Silver linings and all that," she groaned and Phoebe nodded solemnly.

The door to the huge office then opened and slammed closed, and each of them turned to see Warren as he came storming towards them, clearly having been the one who had burst through it. He didn't say a word to any of them. He just charged straight for his small office and shut himself inside. Wynter went to go over to him, but Phoebe stopped her with a gentle hand on her arm.

"Give him a minute," she told her, "if we've all learned something since working with that guy it's not to go barging in when he's in a shitty mood."

"I've a feeling his mood isn't going to improve by me being here," Wynter confided in her with a frown as she watched Warren pace up and down in his small space.

"He seemed distant upstairs. More so than if he was trying to just playing it cool. Have I done something else to upset him?"

"Mr Cole did speak to him last night," Phoebe answered, and she followed Wynter's gaze to where her boss continued to pace like a caged animal. "He told me before how he'd been warned to stay away from you. Do you think something more was said?"

"I guess I'd best find out," Wynter replied with a shrug. She couldn't wait any longer. She had to know what was eating Warren and so walked over to his door and crept inside without so much as knocking.

He turned to her like he was about to rip her head off, but then stopped when he realised it was Wynter there and not one of his usual engineers. Warren just stared at her and then stormed over to his chair and flopped into it with a huff.

"So, how was it?" he demanded as she took a seat opposite him and Wynter frowned.

"How was what?"

"He built you a bedroom, Wynter. A fucking bedroom! Told us all how you were taking so long to get ready because he'd spent the day in your bed with you and the time had run over. I know you said he touches you, but I didn't realise things between the two of you had progressed to him spending the entire day in bed with you."

Oh, so that was why everyone had been looking at her like that. Wynter wanted to scream at Warren for being such a gullible idiot. She wanted to curse him and call him a child. But instead, she calmly straightened in her seat and took a deep breath before leaning closer and placing her hands on the desk between them.

"Firstly, he built me a glorified prison cell," she informed him, flexing her fingers in a bid to stifle the rage still bubbling within her. "And secondly, he always spends the day with me. That's nothing new. However, nothing happened between us. Not like that anyway."

"Then like what?" Warren asked desperately, and she was pleased to see him calming down at last.

"Marcus is evil, Warren. He taunts me. Plays horrible games and watches as I fail with the biggest smile on his goddamn face. Whenever he touches me it isn't to be kind or sensual. It's purely to get what he wants from me."

"I warned you," he replied, but there was no victory in it and Wynter could tell. "Why would he build you a cell?"

"Because I keep defying his orders and he doesn't like it," Wynter told him honestly, "he said he's going to lock me away whenever he pleases and that it's for my own safety."

"As if that makes it okay," Warren answered, and she was glad he seemed to be on the same page. Wynter nodded. "And he really stays with you all day when you're working overtime?"

"Yeah, bar when I'm sleeping. Although sometimes he does stay even then," she answered uncomfortably, but she knew she had to be honest. "Why?"

"I just know he never does that with Jack," Warren answered with a puzzled look on his rugged face. "He told me once how Mr Cole feeds and then sends him down to his office until he's ready for more. Apparently he only feeds about twice or three times a day."

Wynter gulped. How on Earth could the others have it so easy? Was it the same with Joanna too? Surely not. Maybe just with the male managers.

"And what about the others?" she croaked.

"Patrick is obviously a different set up, but I think it's the same for Joanna. I always heard Marcus has meetings during the day so they never stayed upstairs with him. I might be wrong though," Warren said, and he seemed to be growing further concerned the more they spoke. Like her, he was realising there was indeed a big difference to how Marcus treated her when compared to them.

"Shit," she whispered, looking around out the windows at the rest of the team. They were going about their business and not watching them, but still Wynter was anxious. "Do you think he really is different with me?"

"Seems so," he replied, leaning towards her and taking her hand in his. "Which explains why he tried to turn me off you last night. I think he's jealous."

Wynter wanted to laugh. She couldn't fathom how Marcus could possibly be jealous when all he had to do was take what he wanted and neither of them could do a thing about it, but at the same time, it made sense. He had been acting out a lot and been erratic too. Far from how he'd come across during their initial meeting.

"What did he say?"

"He told me about David," Warren replied, and Wynter sat back in her chair as an icy chill swept down her spine.

"Did he tell Phoebe?" she demanded and Warren shook his head no.

"And I won't either. It isn't fair on her," he said, but then he looked away, as if he couldn't quite hold Wynter's gaze.

"Hang on," she asked, "what exactly did he tell you?"

"We all knew David fancied you, Wynter. It makes sense that he would've pursued you and maybe not have been able to handle the rejection. Did he really commit suicide after you turned him down?"

The very insinuation made Wynter so angry she wanted to scream, but instead she reacted by bursting out laughing. It was the crazy kind of laughter that was more shock than amusement, and yet she couldn't stop herself. Not until she put her head in her hands and let her tears come instead. How dare Marcus concoct such a vile lie? She was livid!

"David never went near those stairs, Warren," she told him when she'd calmed down enough to answer. "But I guess it was the best explanation for his so very many injuries."

Warren paled and put his hand over his mouth.

"What injuries?" he asked incredulously.

Wynter shook her head, trying to fight the barrage of images flooding back to her. Especially the memory of David's body flying up and down against the ceiling and then the floor, and the ceiling again. It wouldn't leave her, and she thought it might never.

"Have you ever seen someone die?" she asked Warren, who shook his head no, "it isn't quick, like in the movies. They don't accept their fate and get on with it. Death is more like a drawn out, obstinate thing. Something that you have to commit to forcing upon its intended. The victim makes awful sounds as the pain wracks through them, and it seems to take forever before they're silent and it's over. I never, ever want to see that happen again."

"Marcus did it?" Warren asked, his face now thunderous.

"No," Wynter told him honestly, "David was indeed infatuated with me and he tried to force himself on me, but she saved me. The Priestess killed him to protect me."

"Who?"

Wynter frowned and went to laugh, but then realised he was being serious.

"The Priestess?" she repeated with a wide-eyed look. "You know, red cloak. Deep, weird voice... Marcus's number one loyal crone and all-round badass powerful witch?"

Warren continued to look at her blankly and Wynter shook her head. This couldn't be happening. She was sure he had to know her. He just had to. "Seriously. If you're messing with me I'm going to flip my shit," she told him, but he remained at a loss for words. He clearly had no idea who the Priestess was, and genuinely so.

"I'm sorry," he replied with a shrug, "I've never seen anyone like that around here, or heard anyone speak of her before. That doesn't mean anything though. Maybe Mr Cole only lets you and the other managers see her?"

It made sense, Wynter guessed, and she nodded.

"I hope so," she then told him, "because it's either that or I'm going mad."

ELEVEN

Marcus summoned his Priestess to his office and got a delightful surprise when she appeared to him as Marcella and not in her usual robes.

"My lady," he greeted her with a gentle bow, "how lovely to see you."

"My lord, the feeling is mutual, as always." She stepped closer and hovered for a moment before deciding on having a seat opposite him at the desk.

"How are things going?" Marcus asked her, and he was pleased to see that Marcella knew exactly what he was getting at without him having to outright say it.

"Wynter is indeed an enigma," the witch replied with a fond smile. Marcus didn't know why, but that small smile irked him. Marcella wasn't allowed to care for anyone but him. Like with all his slaves, he was their number one priority, and he wanted to be sure that the same rules would apply to his Priestess as well.

"You care for her," he said. It was a statement rather than a question, and Marcella offered him the slightest nod of her head in agreement.

"But my love is reserved solely for you, my lord," she appeased him, and Marcus immediately calmed. He could sense she was telling the truth and smiled, his eyes flicking down to her stomach and back again.

"And your child," he reminded her. Marcella beamed and nodded.

"Indeed," she replied, instinctively placing a hand over her womb. The baby was still nothing more than an embryo, and yet, Marcus could tell she was going to be a strong witch and a powerful ally in his never-ending crusade for power. Like her mother. And like Marcella, he would treasure and guide the child as if she were his own.

"Have you seen anything more of her future?" he then asked, his mind going back to Wynter and the prophecy Marcella had previously told him.

"I still see her running into the arms of another," she replied with a frown. She then settled back in the seat and stared off into the distance wistfully. "But I cannot see whom. I have made steps with Warren to ensure he stays away from her, but I can only assume it either isn't enough, or that it could possibly not be him."

"But who else?" he enquired and Marcella shrugged. There was no one who Wynter cared for as much as the boy, Marcus had been forced to admit that much, and he had also used her attraction to his advantage to make her stay with him. The feelings between the two were mutual, and yet even Marcus could see they were in no rush to fall in love and plan their escape.

Her curse was lifted and he could see such a difference now between Wynter and the other members of his team. They all adored him, even if they also had undercurrents of loathing or fear, and Marcus liked it that way, however with her it was all just one big show. But the façade was not for him. No, the pretence was for the others. She was already an outsider because of the special attention Marcus gave her, but if the rest of his slaves found out she was also free from his curse Wynter would undoubtedly be ousted entirely. They wouldn't trust her. Either that, or they would envy her. They certainly wouldn't be friendly anymore. Only civil out of courtesy. And then she'd be truly alone. Broken. Marcus smiled to himself, thinking how that might actually be kind of perfect. Something he could implement should the need arise.

"I put a spell on Warren," Marcella told him, her voice plucking him from his reverie, "so that he doesn't sleep with her.

"When did you do that?" he asked, and was impressed with her initiative.

"I rang down on Saturday to ask him to fix my computer. There was nothing wrong with it, of course, but I took him into my office and cast a curse on him. No matter how much he wants her, something will always get between them. Such as yourself and Phoebe when they were hiding themselves away after he'd left my office, or perhaps an idea that will pop into his head and turn him off at the last minute. They'll never get together, my lord. Not as long as my curse still holds."

"But that won't stop her from wanting him, will it?"

"No," Marcella confirmed, "and you cannot kill him or send him away without her seeing it as an offensive move. One to which she will react in kind."

"Wynter cannot be allowed to leave me," Marcus ground. He knew that wasn't Marcella's intention, but she had given him a warning. One he knew without her having to have said the words aloud.

"Then merge with her," the Priestess implored. She then sat forward in her seat and stared into his dark gaze. "Do as your soul is telling you and take her as your own, my lord. You continue to fight your attraction to her and yet I can see it within you. I can sense your yearning."

"Then you are mistaken, my lady," he replied, forcing himself not to strike her or take any action that might result in hurting his darling Priestess, or her child.

"What you sense is lust. Nothing more."

"But, my lord," Marcella began, however Marcus cut her off.

"But nothing. I appreciate your candour as always, however you must learn to hold your tongue when you're proven incorrect," he chided.

Marcella did the right thing—she backed down. She saved them both from having an argument about who was right or wrong, and Marcus was pleased to see she'd not taken her place by his side for granted. He could lock her away just like he had her mother when the time had come for her to drift out of his life and leave the young witch in his care. He was her master. Her tutor. Her mentor. But more than that, he was her everything and Marcella ought to remember so. "What's next?" he asked, giving her the opportunity to prove herself to him again, and the Priestess did not disappoint.

"You're needed at the new club tomorrow to oversee the final arrangements, but that can be done in one day. Afterwards, why not take the opportunity to visit the other new sites? Take her with you. Let her know just why those of your kind require so many new slaves. Teach her why it's important she remains loyal to you, rather than be thrown to the masses."

"You mean, show her the hordes?"

Marcella nodded and a wicked grin spread across her lips.

"She'll soon come running to you once she sees the truth about what happens when the vampire race you so carefully control are left without proper guidance. Make it clear that if she runs, then it's towards a worse danger. Better she stay with the devil she knows, so to speak."

Marcus nodded and he too grinned from ear to ear. The Priestess was right.

If Wynter saw for herself just how terrifying the truth was about the state of his kind she would think twice about trying to evade him again. The vampires had needed a leader and he had taken it upon himself to provide it, but at the same time only those of wealth were afforded the lifestyle his clubs allowed. The rest fed on the scraps their sires threw them and they had become wild, feral creatures of the night because of it. Certainly beings no young woman such as Wynter should ever hope to come across unprotected.

It was indeed a case of her being better off sticking with the evil master she despised, and Marcus was determined to let her see so with her own eyes.

***

Wynter was just finishing up for the night when she got a knock on her office door. She'd hoped to find Warren on the other side, or perhaps Marcella like she had the morning before, but instead it was Bryn. He was standing tall and with that air of arrogance about him she had come to dislike, but Wynter still smiled politely and greeted him regardless. Her personal opinion of him aside, the fact still remained that she would have to work with the guy for the foreseeable future. So, rather than groan and make a comment about how she was now officially off the clock, she beckoned him inside her office, but kept the door open.

"Mr Cole has asked that you go to his office before leaving. He has a favour to ask of you," Bryn told her, and this time she couldn't fight her reaction. Wynter knew all too well about Marcus and his favours and wasn't too keen on walking into some kind of trap.

"What favour?" she tried, but Bryn just shook his head. He either didn't know or wasn't allowed to tell. Either way, Wynter knew there was only one option. She had to go up there, and with the best will in the world, told herself it really was just going to be for a minute or two before she'd be on her merry way again.

She wanted her home and her bed. Some peace and

quiet and, most importantly, some alone time.

Wynter gathered her things and plucked her coat from the hook behind the door. Rather than put it on, she hung it over one arm and hooked her handbag over the other. Bryn was out the door and down the hall before she'd even finished locking up, and had even had the courtesy to call the lift for her so it was sat open at the ready when she reached it.

She felt like calling him a job's worth. Felt like snickering and telling him to stop being such an arse kisser, but instead she forced herself to say nothing at all. Not even a polite thank you.

The lift arrived on the fourth floor within a few seconds and the doors opened to reveal Jack, who was standing over by the window looking down at the street below. Marcus, however, was nowhere to be found and so Wynter took a few tentative steps inside before leaving her things in one of the chairs around the meeting table.

She watched Jack, who had to know she was there, but hadn't turned to greet her at all. He seemed lost in his own thoughts and away with them a little. Nothing like the cocky and arrogant man she'd met when she'd first started the job. Something had happened to him, she just didn't know what.

The sound of the elevator arriving again then made Wynter jump in shock and she turned on her heel to see who was just about to join them. Joanna stepped out of it and she had the smuggest of smiles on her face, but only until she saw the other two managers there as well. Wynter wondered if she'd thought Marcus had summoned her to feed him, and got her answer when Joanna shuffled nervously to button up her blouse and cover herself a little.

Wynter wanted to tell her she could have him. To inform Joanna of all the ways she despised their boss and would gladly never let him feed from her again given the chance. But she couldn't do it. She couldn't break her promise and also allow for her façade to be uncovered. She had chosen to live this lie and knew she couldn't go back on it now.

"Where's our master?" Joanna demanded and Wynter ignored her. She instead went over to where a small fridge held bottled drinks and snacks to keep Marcus's workers hydrated and refuelled, and she plucked herself a bottle of ice cold water. She was still gulping it down when he finally appeared from inside his now fully privately partitioned area and grinned around at them.

"So glad you could all make it," he then chimed, "please, follow me."

Marcus walked back to where he'd come from and Wynter's stomach began to churn. She didn't want to go back there. She wanted to be back in that lift and on her way home already, and yet, there was nothing she could do to refuse him. Like always, Marcus was going to get his damn way, whether she agreed with it or not.

Joanna practically ran for the door, while Jack's pace was far slower and matched Wynter's. She let the pair of them go on ahead and then hovered in the doorway, watching them from a few feet away while she made up her mind about whether to follow them or not. "Wynter, come." Marcus held out his hand to her and she scowled back at him. He had no such power to command her body like that and they both knew it, but he was exerting a different level of control. One she couldn't ignore or fight against if she wanted to keep up with the pretence of her still being under his spell.

She did as he commanded and took the seat Marcus offered her beside Jack and Joanna on the new sofa. Only when they were each perched beneath his gaze did he speak again. "The four of us are going to be doing some travelling," he told them.

Joanna reacted with a shriek of delight and she even

clapped her hands excitedly, like some teenager who'd just been told the next school trip was to fucking Lapland. Jack simply nodded to Marcus and otherwise sat motionless and silent. Wynter shook her head but bit her tongue. What she wanted to say about his offer would be best done in private.

"When? Where?" Joanna asked, still bouncing in her seat.

"Tomorrow," Marcus replied and he put his hand out for Joanna to take before pulling her up out of her seat. "Now, go home and pack some things, and bring them with you to work this evening. We leave this time tomorrow." Joanna nodded profusely and then skipped away, and Marcus then turned his attention to Jack, whom Wynter knew was working his overtime days so probably wouldn't be in any rush to try and go. She was surprised to find him quite the opposite.

"I'll make a list of the things I need and head home right away, Mr Cole. I'll be back in time to feed you before six o'clock."

"Yes, you do that," Marcus agreed and then Jack left without another word.

Wynter was left gobsmacked. She knew for sure now how their vampire boss really did treat them each so differently. Jack was, for all intents and purposes, on duty for the day, and yet he'd been allowed to go home? That wasn't fair at all, and when they were alone, Wynter told Marcus so.

"Why is it Jack gets to go home during the day? I thought he was feeding you today?"

"Simple," Marcus answered with a nonchalant wave of his hand, "it's because I only usually feed from him once or twice. Perhaps a pint or so, nothing more. I only need a little really."

Wynter opened and closed her mouth in shock. How dare he take so much from her and so little from the others? Again that voice was ringing in her head about

EDEN WILDBLOOD

how it wasn't fair. None of this was.

"So it's true?" she demanded, recoiling when Marcus sat down beside her, pinning her in. "You treat the women differently to the men."

"I suppose," he answered without a care, nor did he seem to feel the need to apologise for it. "But Joanna is different as well. You know how much she cares for me, but it's so profound that her blood is sickly sweet. Some days just a sip will suffice."

Wynter shook her head, glowering at Marcus. All the bites he'd given her and all the blood he had taken. He'd almost drained her dry on more than one occasion and now she had to hear this? It made her sick.

"If only I loved you as much as she does," she mused aloud, "you might leave me alone too."

"I'm counting on you to never love me, Wynter," he told her with a small chuckle, "and if you ever do, I'll soon beat that love right out of you. That's what I do to Joanna when she's been naughty or has displeased me. I force her to fear me. I beat the sense back into her and then drink my fill while she's broken and beaten down. But I don't need to do that with you, do I? You despise me and reek of loathing and bitterness every minute of every day. It's intoxicating," Marcus added, and he breathed her in as if to make it clear he could sense her hatred even still.

All of her instincts told her to run. To flee and never return, but anxiety speared in her gut at the sheer thought of running from him. Marcus wouldn't let her go, she knew this, but she would continue to fight, even if that was what he wanted.

"I'm going home, Marcus," Wynter told him as she fought her way out of her seat and to her feet. "I'll grab some things for the trip and bring them with me this evening, just like the others. And I expect to be paid overtime for while we are away."

Marcus burst out laughing and shook his head as

though she'd not only amused him greatly, but also surprised him. Wynter scowled down at him and balled her hands into fists. "Today is not my overtime day and neither is tomorrow, or the next two. You cannot expect me to stay."

"It's not that," he explained, although still chuckling to himself. "It's just that you are too innocuous for your own good sometimes, Wynter."

"And what's that supposed to mean?" she cried.

Marcus was up and out of his seat in less than a second and he stormed forwards, closing the distance between them in a heartbeat. Wynter wanted to stand her ground but she couldn't. Her feet moved backwards one step at a time in retreat and before she knew it she'd hit the wall behind.

With a grin, he boxed her in with his hands either side and then pressed his body against hers. He was taking deep, languid breaths and she knew he was still relishing in her bitterness and fear.

"What I mean is that you *are* home, my sweet. This is your home now."

"No fucking way," Wynter cried, trying to fight his hold, but Marcus remained where he was and shook his head as though still highly amused by her.

"Your house has been sold and your things cleared out. I've taken the liberty of putting them in storage for you to sort at a later date," he explained without even a hint of a care for having invaded her personal space and taking measures she had not okayed.

"You can't do that!" she screamed, punching her still balled fists against his chest in her angst. Neither her pleas nor her punches were getting her anywhere though and Wynter felt like crying. She wanted to scream and bellow at him some more for overstepping the mark by a huge amount, but she actually felt weaker by the moment. She was beginning to wilt under the pressure he insisted on piling up on her.

She was tired and angry, and tired of being angry all the time. All she wanted was some peace and quiet and space from him. Couldn't he at least give her that?

"I can do whatever I want, my sweet," Marcus countered with a smile, "if I say you're staying here permanently, then that's what you'll do. End of discussion."

"Then I'll run away," she tried, but it was an empty threat.

"And who would help you, hmm? The boy under my spell? The Priestess whose loyalty is pledged solely to me?" Marcus put his palms around her shoulders and squeezed, watching her intently with that sinister smile still lingering on his pale face. "Face it, if you leave then I shall consider your actions as an act of war. Our deal will be broken and I'll go right downstairs and snap Warren's neck in front of all his subordinates and make them watch. And then I'll go after each and every one of your friends and family. My men will defile them and mutilate their bodies beyond recognition, and it will be all your fault…"

Wynter's heart broke at the sheer thought of it, and she knew Marcus could tell because his handsome face spread into another of his awful smiles. "There it is. See? I don't even have to torture you, Wynter. You think you're brave and tough, but look how easily you break. Now, go to your room." He pointed to the bedroom she'd been confined to the day before and Wynter shook her head no. She didn't want to be locked away in there all day again.

"No, please," she tried.

"Shall I make you?" Marcus challenged in response, but she shook her head again. She didn't have the energy to fight any longer and knew she couldn't handle being punished.

"I made you a deal and intend to keep my promise. I'll come back, just like I did last week. Please, leave me be. Let me have some freedom," she whimpered as a last ditch attempt to sway him.

Marcus seemed about to cut her down again but then stopped. He eyed her for a couple of seconds, as though reading more than just her emotions, and then seemed to make up his mind.

"I won't lock you in," he countered, "bar my comings and goings, the office door will remain locked and will not be opened again until six o'clock. You are to remain here and are free to use the facilities and kitchen, however I must insist you sleep in your bed and not on the sofa."

"And the bedroom door?" she had to ask, needing to hear him promise her that he wasn't going to lock her inside again.

"Will remain unlocked—for now."

This wasn't what Wynter wanted at all but she was too exhausted to argue any more. She promised herself that when they returned from the trip she would find a way to get back home and away from Marcus's reach day and night. She was entitled to her space and would fight for it, but not today. She desperately needed rest and was willing to concede if it meant she got it.

"I'll stay, for the time being," she told him, "but you're going to have to learn to trust me. I refuse to stay locked up in this club day and night. That wasn't the deal."

"We'll see..."

TWELVE

Wynter slept almost the entire day and while it was nice for Marcus to be able to get a decent amount of work done in the knowledge she was safely locked away, he couldn't help but continue to think of her. He wondered what she might be dreaming of, or if perhaps those dreams were nightmares.

Did she really despise him through and through? She'd told him so and he'd acted in ways to ensure it, but there was still that niggling sense of wonder in the pit of his stomach that told him he was taking the harder route by refusing his feelings and not following his soul's desire by merging with her.

At least if he did, Wynter would be his until death parted them. No other would tear them asunder and he wouldn't have to try so damn hard to make her hate him, because he would instead revel in her adoration and return it tenfold. But it just wasn't his way. Part of him considered reaching out to Camilla and satisfying his carnal hunger with her in a bid to distract himself, but each time he reached for his phone to call upon her, he put it back down.

Jack arrived back at the office early as arranged, and

Marcus led him through to the back rooms and deposited him on the sofa where the three managers had been sat earlier that morning. Wynter was up and in the shower, and while Jack was clearly surprised to find she'd stayed the day there, he didn't ask any questions. He was a good boy like that, and while he saw all, he also didn't feel the need to interfere. Just another reason why Marcus was so fond of him, even still.

Marcus joined him and snapped his fingers to command his Blood Slave to tend to him. He didn't need to say a word. Jack did as was needed and repositioned himself on the sofa so that he could offer his wrist to Marcus for feeding. He accepted, and sliced through his flesh to the veins beneath before taking the first gulp of metallic goodness into his mouth.

He then swirled the blood around his tongue, savouring the taste and sensing all the innermost emotions Jack was dealing with. His slave was still yearning for the touch of his Priestess, but he would never know her body again and Marcus could tell Jack was struggling to come to terms with it. He wanted her and often thought of the virgin he had made love to, having imagined her tight body around his while taking care of his personal needs in private, rather than with their master watching over them. He, like Joanna, had no one he wanted enough to take her place. No one more than the object of his desire and so nothing else would do. Only masturbation and his days spent wallowing in his misery.

As Marcus drew a second gulp, Wynter emerged from the bathroom dressed only in a towel. She jumped in shock at the sight of the pair of them and looked like she might be about to apologise, but then evidently thought better of it and scuttled to her room without comment.

He drew a third mouthful and watched her with hungry, lustful eyes. He saw the smallest curve of her bottom as she passed them and ground his jaw against the flesh between his teeth.

Jack let out a cry of pain but Marcus did not yield. He settled his slave with a wave of power through their bond, exerting control over his body with ease, and Jack fell silent. He was giving off fear in droves though, only exciting the vampire more, and he took another gulp.

Marcus then looked up and caught sight of Wynter in her bedroom. She had the door wide open and was parading around in just a bra and knickers. Did she know they could see her? Marcus had to wonder if she'd thought she'd closed it enough to obscure her from sight, but it was the exact opposite.

Even so, he watched her, desperate to touch that flesh and to taste the delicious nectar coursing beneath it. He gulped harder and harder, ignoring the struggle from the slave beside him. Marcus was ravenous for more and would not relinquish his hold.

He took another gulp, and another, watching as Wynter slid a pretty dress over her head and then let it cascade down over her slim body. It bunched at her curved waist and she wiggled her hips to release it, making him laugh.

The curve of his mouth separated man from monster and Jack's arm fell into his lap with a limp thud. He had been drained to a dangerous point, but would live, and so Marcus left him to rest. Instead, he went to her, his perfect slave, and blocked the doorway with his huge frame.

Wynter turned to glare at him and then looked behind to where Jack lay slumped and half-dead on the sofa.

"I thought you said you only take a little bit from him?" she asked, her voice barely more than a whisper. "He looks half-dead."

Marcus licked his lips and he saw her eyes dart to them. Her cheeks then flushed as some sordid thought went through her mind and he grinned. So, her dreams hadn't been nightmares after all. She was hot and giving off a needy vibe that told him she'd had dreams of a steamy variety and not offloaded any of that need herself while in bed or in her shower.

Why wait? He wondered, and then got his answer when he walked inside her room and closed the door behind him. Wynter tried to hide it, but she was definitely scared. Not necessarily of him, but of the closed door. That was why she'd left it open rather than maintain some modesty after her shower, and probably why she'd not felt comfortable enough to take care of business after her long rest.

"You need something, don't you, my sweet?" Marcus asked, stepping closer, and he adored the flush of Wynter's cheeks as she tried to lie to him.

"No, now would you please open the door."

"No," he echoed, sauntering closer. Wynter backed up like she had earlier that morning and he advanced, closing the distance in no time at all and then boxing her into the corner.

Without a word he then lifted her skirt and pressed the flat of his palm over her mound. Wynter groaned and sucked in a breath, like she was going to say something, but Marcus put his other hand directly over her mouth and pressed it closed. His thoughts were wild and frenzied, but his actions smooth as he slid his thumb under the waistband of her knickers and then pushed them down. The sheer fabric glided downwards and slid around her ankles with ease, leaving Wynter naked at the waist. She moaned again when he stroked his way down over her barely-there tuft of hair towards her clit.

Marcus shushed her and pinned her harder against the wall, teasing open her thighs by splaying his fingers wide and Wynter followed his command without complaint. She even arched her hips to grant him easier access, and Marcus laughed to himself as he thought about all the times she had defied him. Told him she hated him. And now here she was, soaked and ready for him to be inside of her.

He started slowly, teasing his way in and out and then taking a second to rub her clit with each withdrawal. Wynter was breathing hard through her nose and began arching her hips in time with each of his plunges, as if she'd figured out his rhythm, so Marcus altered it. He pressed his long fingers all the way inside and pushed against her g-spot, making her moan and buck and tense around him, and laughed again. "I can do this for you every day if only you be my good, good girl," he whispered against her temple, running his teeth over the top of her forehead as his desire to take a bite grew stronger. He pushed in again and tickled that same spot, this time offering relentless pressure that he knew would force her over the edge.

Wynter's eyes grew wide and she suddenly gripped Marcus by the wrist of the hand between her thighs and pushed it against her, deepening his intrusion. She writhed against it and then came, and he watched her with relish as she reached her climax and came utterly undone.

But it wasn't good enough. He wanted more. Marcus removed the hand covering her mouth and kissed her, ravishing her lips with his wild mouth and then he bit down on her bottom lip, drawing blood. He then drank her down and continued to kiss her, while Wynter's body went into overdrive and she began to shudder with another almighty release. Her core clenched around him, but Marcus continued to push in and out at the speed Wynter still dictated thanks to her hands doing the guiding.

When she was finally over that precipice and fully spent, her hands fell limply at her sides and she trembled against him. Marcus wondered if she would fall in a heap should he let go, and again he contemplated doing so, but then thought better of it. Instead, he ordered his hand to retreat from within her still throbbing body and pulled his mouth away from hers.

Then, he scooped Wynter up off her feet and carried her to the bed, where he laid her down atop the duvet and watched as she basked in the euphoric afterglow of her releases.

***

Wynter wanted to tell Marcus to leave, but not for any reason other than because she felt vulnerable and laid bare in the aftermath of what'd just happened. She didn't want to admit it to him, but she'd enjoyed that. Like, really enjoyed it. It'd been so long since her last proper session in the bedroom that she felt like she'd forgotten what a penis looked like, but couldn't deny his hands had worked some serious magic in place of her having had a proper seeing to.

He'd been right, she had been horny as hell, but hadn't known how best to deal with it. The bathroom had reminded her of her embarrassing attempt to seduce Marcus the week before, so she hadn't felt like getting herself off while in there, and so she'd figured the bedroom would have to do. But then she'd emerged and found Marcus feeding on Jack on the sofa rather than the privacy she'd anticipated. It was a strange sight and something which had stirred a variety of emotions in her. Yes, there was the usual shock and sense of *yuk*, but there was something else too. Marcus's eyes had been full of heat and she'd felt them on her, but there was also a certain kind of sexiness to watching him feed. Something she'd never considered before. He was powerful and like a gory king among men. Wynter had gone to her room and thought of nothing more as she'd gotten dressed and as soon as he'd appeared in the doorway, she knew he'd figured her out.

The big bad wolf had come to claim his prize, and for some reason, Wynter had wanted nothing more than for him to take it.

"You fed from me," she whispered, licking her swollen lips and breaking the silence at last.

"Yes, it appears I did," Marcus replied in a mirthful tone, "how very naughty of me…"

"You should be punished," she teased, watching him from under her lashes. Wynter felt tired again in spite of her having gotten an entire nine hours of sleep, but knew it was just her body's way of enjoying the aftermath of her sexual release. It would pass, and so too would their moment of playing nice, and so Wynter was determined to enjoy both while they lasted.

"I could drink from you every day," he replied as he lifted her dress and gazed down at her still naked core. "And I could touch you like that every day too. If only you'd be mine and no other's. And if you proved your loyalty to me and did everything I asked without argument."

"Never gonna happen," she replied with a smile, but then faltered when she realised he was being serious. Wynter lifted herself up onto her elbows and peered down at him, watching as he covered her back up and then plucked her knickers from the floor.

"Put these on," he ordered, and was back to being icy cold again.

Wynter did as he'd asked, and then she clambered off the edge of the bed and blocked the door, staring up into his immense blue eyes.

"Whatever you think and whatever you do, I will always be my own person, Marcus. What you have to realise is that it's not a bad thing to let a woman have her own thoughts and feelings. You might actually like being part of the modern world if only you'd give it a try."

He moved her out of the way by physically lifting her up by the shoulders and placing her back down a couple of feet away.

Marcus didn't seem to be angry with her, but he also appeared to have considered the conversation over with, so Wynter let him go and she instead took off for the bathroom to freshen up again and do her hair and makeup. She also had to finish packing, so got straight to it, putting the thoughts of him and his promise of some kind of future aside, for now.

THIRTEEN

Wynter wasn't sure exactly what she'd expected of their trip, but a drive to the other side of the city in a blacked out minibus wasn't exactly it. She had to admit though, it wasn't a thing like the tin can style old buses she'd been in before. This one was state of the art and more than comfortable enough, but she'd figured Marcus for more of a sports car type. Or maybe one of those huge armoured cars she'd seen diplomats drive around in. Something exciting and that reeked of importance, not a standard *human* mode of transport.

She tried not to watch him as they drove, but it was hard given how they were sitting directly opposite one another in the back. Jack was to her left and Bryn to her right, but Joanna had been quick and had made sure she'd taken the seat beside their master before anyone else could.

Wynter hadn't minded one little bit, but now wished she had chosen another seat because all she could feel was his gaze on her. The look in his eye brought back all kinds of sordid thoughts and memories of what'd just happened in her so-called bedroom and she found herself growing warm. Marcus had touched her in ways he hadn't ever before. He'd been soft and gentle, and oddly adoring. He'd touched her like a lover, not a controlling oppressor, and she'd come away confused and still scared, but also eager for more of that touch.

When they arrived at their destination—the location of Marcus's new nightclub *Bound*—they were each given a hard hat and a high-visibility jacket to wear, and then were shown around the new club. It was so close to being done that they were already stocking the shelves behind the bar area, but upstairs there was still building and decorating work going on and the team trailed along behind Marcus as he led them around, pointing to each of the departments and offices explaining what they were to become. Wynter couldn't understand why he felt the need to though, as it was almost an exact replica of the offices back at *Slave*. She knew before he told them which were the HR offices and such, and recognised the four private offices along the hallway as soon as they arrived beside them.

"My dear managers," Marcus barked as he came to a stop, "you will oversee both clubs so might have to visit with me again on a regular basis. Here are your offices should you require some private space. Your key will open both locks."

"Master," Joanna jumped in, sidling closer and fluttering her eyelashes up at him. "Will we stay here some days too?"

"You, my darling," Marcus answered, and Wynter hated how she felt a twinge of jealousy in her gut when he placed a hand against the small of Joanna's back, "shall come with me. Wherever I am, you managers are to follow. Plain and simple."

"As will I, I presume?" Bryn asked and Wynter had to hide her smile at the jealous edge to his tone. So, someone else had felt that twinge too?

"Indeed," Marcus agreed and then he led them upstairs to where the final touches were being put on his office. It was the same setup as he'd originally had back at *Slave* and Wynter had to swallow a lump in her throat when she looked down at the ground at where David's body had lain in a crumpled heap in the other, previously matching office. Everything was exactly the same and Wynter hoped Marcus would change it like he had the other one. She didn't much like being reminded of what'd happened, even if it hadn't been here.

"Ladies and gents," chimed a woman's voice from across the huge room and they each turned to watch as a tall brunette came sauntering towards them, teetering on ridiculously high heels considering the place was still technically a building site. She came to a stop in front of their master and kissed his cheek. "Marcus, darling. I wasn't expecting you until tomorrow morning. I had intended to lay on a feast in your honour. My sire will be most displeased with me."

"You know as well as I do, Claudine that I do not feed from the slaves in my employ, only my managers." He beckoned to the three of them with his hand and Claudine, presumably a fellow vampire, turned to eye each of them in turn.

Wynter picked up on the woman's distaste for the four of them and refused to look away when under her scrutiny like the others had done. As far as she was aware, she had no orders to act timid or fearful of the others of Marcus's kind. She would give respect to those who reciprocated it, but she wouldn't shy away. He'd protect her and keep her safe, she was sure of it, and so stood her ground.

"This one reeks of self-importance, Marcus," the woman told him with a sneer, "makes me sick."

"Yes," he replied without a care for the insult she'd just administered. "And Jack there is heartbroken and desperately lonely, while Joanna is an insufferable bore who adores me so much I can beat her within an inch of her life and she'll always come back for more. They each serve their purposes, dear. Much like you serve yours."

Wynter felt like applauding him for the comeback but settled instead for the tiniest of smiles. She didn't want to push her luck, after all.

She then stared down at the bracelet still around her wrist. The gift from the Priestess. She'd never taken it off and didn't want to either, and thought it odd how it had just become part of herself. Something she was so used to she forgot it was even there. It had to be magical. The black mist swirling within the single dark bead was mesmerising and Wynter had often found herself staring into it. It was marvellous. Like now, was it somehow getting darker? It seemed so.

"Ah yes, back to the task at hand," Claudine then said, and Wynter snapped out of her reverie at the sound. She then watched as the vampire turned her attention back to Marcus and ignored both his answer and his slaves. "The last of the work is due to be finished well ahead of schedule and Camilla has agreed to your request for funding of her hordes' feeding days. She does wish to speak with you to go over the terms, though, and has requested that you visit with her immediately."

Wynter watched as a frown encroached on Marcus's usually so carefully stoic guise, and she got the feeling he didn't much fancy going to visit this Camilla, whoever she was. Wynter thought back to the apparition she'd seen, though. Could that be her? Or perhaps, someone associated with her? She was willing to bet this trip had to be the first step in her being set free of Marcus, though. It was too much of a coincidence otherwise.

They were finally away from *Slave* and due to travel with him for however long he determined, and while things had indeed changed between them, Wynter still yearned to be released from his tight grip. Still wanted to meet the woman who had appeared to her and find out the truth behind her promise of an option-number-three.

Claudine then took the small group through the last of the walkthrough and finally she ushered them all into a small office just inside the main front doors. There, the humans were offered refreshments while the two vampires talked in private over to one side of the room.

Wynter wasn't sure why, but something about the set up didn't feel right. She sipped on her freshly brewed coffee and stared out the window to the foyer beyond, watching as the workmen went about their business as usual. None of them appeared to be hiding anything or watching from over their shoulders, so she turned her attention back to the room and realised the source of her unease was in there with them. Claudine. She had been employed by Marcus to be Project Manager of the new club's opening, so he had to trust her, but there was something off about the vampire. Something that made Wynter's blood run cold whenever she looked at her.

As she continued to watch, an odd sensation began to creep up her spine and she suddenly felt lightheaded. She tried to shake the feeling off, but then looked around at the others and realised that they too seemed to be reacting in the same way. It was like when Marcus had drugged her using his cronies at the bar. One moment, Wynter was with it, and the next her legs were so tremendously tired they buckled and she slumped to her knees. The others each did the same as well and it wasn't long before they were in a heap together on the floor of the office, barely fighting to stay awake.

The last thing Wynter remembered was watching as Claudine turned to them with a smile, while Marcus was grimacing.

***

"About time," Claudine told Marcus, who was

seething at her audacity but had decided to keep his cool, at least for the time being. "My witch cast that spell before we'd even walked into this office. Your humans are strong to have taken this long to succumb."

"And you are on dangerous ground," he answered curtly, "I do not appreciate my staff being mistreated this way. It's not how I like to do things."

"Oh really?" Claudine responded with a smirk, "Jakob tells it a little differently…"

Marcus sneered. Of course that little sneak was behind this coup. His information regarding what he'd seen at Marcus's office had clearly gone back to his mistress, who had now sent her witch across during his visit to ensure he accepted her request for an audience.

Only the same witch who cast the spell to knock his three slaves and assistant out could undo this sort of spell and Marcus didn't need to be told so to figure out that her actions formed an ultimatum. Attend or have naught but a pile of sleeping humans to drag back across the city. The rest of them he'd willingly leave as such, but not his favourite little pet. Not Wynter. He wanted to curse and lash out at Claudine as well as his surroundings, but forced his rage aside. He would save it for the real culprit. Camilla.

"Let's away then," he barked, but first did not pass up the opportunity to grab Claudine by her throat and pin her to the wall behind. "And if you ever try something like this again, do rest assured that I will not hesitate to rip you to pieces and burn the remains. I care not for whom you serve. When you're employed by me, you're mine to command."

She tried to loosen Marcus's grip but he refused to relinquish his hold, squeezing tighter. He wanted her to know he meant what he'd said. It was no idle threat.

When he eventually let go it was because he'd chosen to, and nothing more. "Now, take me to your sire."

FOURTEEN

When Wynter awoke, her head was pounding and it made opening her eyes almost too difficult to even bother with. It was as if she'd been hit in the head or something, because everything from the neck up seemed to hurt like a bitch. What the hell was in that coffee? And why had yet another vampire felt the need to spike hers and the others' drinks to make them go easily? Couldn't that bitch have simply asked?

She wondered though if the drugs hadn't been about getting the three of them to behave, but to garner the attention of someone else. Someone tall and handsome with those icy blue eyes. Thinking of Marcus only made Wynter's head hurt more and so she buried it in the pillow someone had thankfully placed beneath her and groaned.

"The affects will wear off soon, Wynter," a deep and heavily accented voice told her, and she mumbled in response about how it wasn't wearing off soon enough, making the man watching over her laugh.

She knew the voice before she even had to open her eyes. It was that strange vampire from the night of David's death. Jakob.

"Where am I?" she asked when she was indeed beginning to feel a little better. "And where are the others?" she added, having noticed how quiet the room was.

"You are the only one Camilla is interested in, so the others were left behind to await Marcus's return. You won't be joining him," a second voice told her, and it was one Wynter recognised as well, but not from any meeting. No, she knew this woman from the night she had come to her as a vision.

She jumped up and looked to where the sound had come from, blinking away the sleep from her dry eyes. Lo and behold, the woman who had appeared to her before was indeed there with them. She was whole. Flesh and blood.

Wynter looked from the woman to Jakob and back, checking that she was safe to talk openly, and breathed a sigh when the woman nodded and offered her a kind smile.

"You're the one who came to me. You told me to follow him to you and that you'd separate us. Is that offer still on the table?"

"It is indeed," the woman confirmed with a knowing smile, "I'm pleased you were able to refuse his advances. It speaks volumes about your strength of will, Wynter. I intend to follow through on the promise I made you, but it won't come easily. You have to know what you're letting yourself in for before we attempt this."

She wanted to tell the woman a resounding yes, but then hesitated. Her feelings towards Marcus had changed over the past few days. She had changed. Him too. She wasn't as desperate to leave him as she had been before and couldn't actually offer the witch a definite answer. She needed to get her head straight first.

"We'll give you some time to think about it, Wynter," Jakob interjected, making her smile with the way he said her name as *Vinter*. "Marcus is busy for now so we have time to allow the details to sink in."

The witch looked furious with him for having stalled the proceedings and Wynter frowned, thinking that if this really was all for her benefit then what did it matter if they waited just a little longer? The woman's actions told her there had to be another motive at hand, and she wanted to know what it was before she acted out against Marcus and potentially lost her place with him forever.

"Yes, I'd like some time to think," she answered him and then turned to the witch, "will you tell me more later when my head isn't pounding?"

"Sure," she replied with an icy edge to her tone that made Wynter retreat even further. The witch then stood and stormed out of the room, and Wynter half expected Jakob to join her, but he didn't. He simply sat back in his chair and watched her with an amused smile.

"You gonna tell me what's really going on here?" she asked him as she lay back on the bed and stared up at the ceiling. Her head really was still pounding and it was irking her, making her grouchy. "Why the rush? And what does she really have to gain by separating us?"

Jakob was quiet for a moment, as though deliberating on just how much to reveal, but then he shrugged and began to speak. It was as if he didn't care about the repercussions for telling her the truth and while she didn't want him to get in any trouble, Wynter was glad of his candour.

"Lola works solely for the love of her mistress, like your Priestess does her master. The vampire Camilla has asked her to separate the pair of you. Of course, she intends to follow through on her promise to deliver, but cannot break his witch's spell by force. That's why she came to you when your soul was crying out for a way to escape Marcus's clutches, because you have to be willing…"

Jakob leaned forward, placing his elbows on his knees and Wynter felt him glaring at her, reading her reactions in exactly the same way Marcus always did. He was so intense.

She wondered if perhaps all vampires could read humans so easily, and decided to be more careful which of them she put her trust in. Wynter turned and looked into Jakob's eyes, and was surprised to find warmth in the deep blue hues. Far from the iciness behind Marcus's. He wasn't like him at all, and it was refreshing to discover how not all vampires were devious and selfish megalomaniacs like her boss.

"And now that things are different?" she asked him as she turned onto her side and continued to watch him.

"She's scathing. I believe she thought this was going to be easy," Jakob answered, and Wynter frowned.

"Why are you telling me all this?"

"Because I try to be beholden to no one other than myself and I made an oath not to lie," Jakob replied with a soft smile she was once again drawn to, "I get results, Wynter. Make no mistake about that. But, I do it with honour rather than by being devious."

Jakob had a solemn look on his face that made her want to believe him. And to trust that he'd always be honest. She was reminded of him holding her close in an attempt to do the right thing by her once before. And of how he'd stared at her afterwards and had seemed to be peering right into her soul. Was it the truth he was seeking then too? Had he found it?

"So you'll tell me the truth about all of this? About what Camilla wants from me and why?"

"Of course, and I'd appreciate it if you did the same in return. Tell me the truth about what Marcus is up to in his tower. I snooped around that night I found you, but I would like to know first hand what it is he's playing at. What his end goal is," Jakob countered, but Wynter shook her head.

"All I know is that he rules us all with an iron fist. He expects each of his slaves to behave and serve him without question. We don't get told the gory details."

"And yet you fight him, don't you?" Jakob replied with a knowing smile, "everyone else tells him yes while you tell him no. Did you break his curse?"

Wynter looked away. She'd kept that a secret and wasn't sure she wanted to confirm or deny it, regardless of Jakob's request for honesty.

He already knew the answer though, she could tell, and seemed to take her silence as confirmation anyway. "Why do you stay if you already have your freedom? Do you genuinely care for him?"

Wynter knew he couldn't understand. She barely could herself and breathed a sigh.

"I don't know. There are times when he makes me feel good and shows kindness, but there are others when he's a monster who delights in tormenting me. I stay because I have no other choice," she eventually answered, and was surprised to find understanding on Jakob's face.

"Do you think he cares for you? That he could ever love you?" he asked.

"Sometimes. But if he did, surely he wouldn't be so cruel?" Wynter replied, and it dawned on her as she spoke the words that Marcus couldn't possibly love her.

It didn't matter what his eyes showed her when she got too close, his actions were what spoke volumes and he didn't treat her like someone he loved, but someone he wanted to control and have at his command. Just like all his other minions, and yet undoubtedly sweeter because she wasn't under his spell like they were. A true prisoner, just like he'd always wanted.

"Did he threaten you to make you stay?" Jakob asked, continuing on with his interrogation, and she nodded. "Who is it? Which life is at stake if you leave?"

"Everyone I care about," she breathed, and a tear

slid down her temple. "But the first on his hit list is a another of his slaves. Someone I've come to care a great deal about."

"Would this slave do the same for you?" the vampire pressed, and Wynter wanted to say yes, but she actually wasn't convinced he would, in all honesty.

Warren had blown hot and cold too and she had told herself he would only ever sell her out because of his curse, but could never be entirely sure. He wanted out, it was clear, and Wynter wondered if he'd gladly throw her under the bus to save himself given the chance. "It strikes me," Jakob said, breaking her reverie, "that everyone seems to care for you, Wynter. You're likeable and kind, and of course very beautiful, but that's where the fondness ends. You've held back from getting too close to anyone for so long that you've become nothing but a shell. Someone unlovable because you have no heart."

His words hit her like a punch to the chest.

"Don't say that!" she cried and sat up atop the bed. Wynter couldn't imagine him saying anything more hurtful than he just had done and she began to cry. "I'm not *that* closed off and I'm certainly not heartless."

He watched her come undone with a sad expression on his face, but Jakob didn't take back what he'd said.

"You care, it's true," he agreed, "but if you stopped shutting out your emotions you'd see that real connections aren't something you should have to work so hard for. None of these men love you, Wynter. If they did they would put you first without question. They would think of you with their every waking moment and want to spend it by your side. Not play games or leave you guessing whether or not they would make sacrifices to save you."

"So what, I've got to accept that no one loves me and probably never will?" she answered despondently, and hung her head in her hands.

"You can choose. Continue on as you are and let everyone you care about walk all over you because they cannot see you for anything more than you already are. Half a person, and half a heart. Or, open your heart fully and follow it. Don't give up on yourself and go forward in the knowledge that you're more than good enough. That you should be loved. That you deserve to be."

"Fool me once, shame on you."

"Fool me twice, shame on me," Jakob finished for her, and Wynter began to cry harder. She truly was the fool. She had been played time and again because she'd stayed too closed off to see what the people around her were doing. They were using her. Forcing her to do as they wanted by toying with her and manipulating her. And all the while she'd let them because she hadn't wanted to get too close and let anyone hurt her again. Well, no more.

She was going to love with everything she had, and was going to start by learning to love herself again.

Jakob stayed with Wynter for hours. They talked through her past with her ex, Dominic, and how she'd ended up at the club that night when David had approached her. She told him how Marcus had lured her in and then put her under his spell, but how she'd managed to get out of it again.

It felt incredible to finally tell someone. She felt she could trust him and knew that while her admissions weren't secrets he'd keep safe, Jakob seemed to understand her motives. He also appeared to want her to come out of this different and in one strong piece, and it was refreshing being open and completely honest with someone about what she'd been through and how it'd all made her feel.

She wanted to stay there all night, thanks to how comfortable and refreshing it was in his presence. But of course, thanks to the time that'd passed, it wasn't long before her stomach began rumbling and Wynter stood, heading for the doorway.

"I need some food, and quick. Are you taking me for something to eat or shall I see if Lola can bring room service?" she joked, making him laugh. With a smile, Jakob climbed to his feet, opened the door, and then ushered her forward with a wave of his hand.

"Please, after you," he said and then led her out into a dark hallway.

There, Wynter stopped dead thanks to the stark coldness outside. It was far from welcoming. There were doors all the way down the hall they were now in, but each was closed, presumably locked tight. All Wynter could see was the stream of moonlight coming in from the window at the end, and in its cool rays was the path to an exit.

The door she and Jakob had just left through closed with a bang behind them and she jumped, moving closer to him for safety. It was odd how after just a short period of time together she already trusted him so much. But really, she figured why not. He'd been the first person to truly be honest with her and not lie or cheat his way into her good graces, and he certainly hadn't manipulated his way in either. He was strong and seemed to know how to use that strength wisely, and she felt safer by his side.

She peered up into his face and took him in, and watched as the shadows clung to his strong, square jaw and prominent cheekbones. He was looking right back at her, his pale blue eyes roving over her face curiously too. For a few seconds, they simply stood there, taking one another in, and Wynter couldn't deny feeling warmed from the inside out thanks to his closeness. Jakob truly was a handsome, powerful man. His blond hair and blue eyes might make anyone else think of him as a pretty-boy, but she knew differently. She could see the strength behind those eyes and the fierceness in his stance. He was old and wise, and had seen his share of both good and bad. But unlike Marcus, he hadn't sought power or riches. He seemed to want nothing more than balance and peace, hence his openness and ready honesty. A true conundrum.

A shiver then swept down her spine. It was eerily quiet wherever they were and Wynter realised then how she'd quickly gotten used to the sounds of the nightclub around her day and night. She wasn't used to the silence any more and wasn't all that sure she particularly liked it.

"Where to?" Wynter quickly asked and Jakob shrugged.

"Where do humans like to eat?"

She giggled and shook her head.

"There must be a kitchen or something around here? Doesn't Camilla keep human slaves?" she asked, and then paled when Jakob shook his head no.

"She feeds and then gives the scraps to her hordes. Needless to say we don't entertain much…"

"Whoa," Wynter replied, and it was hard to shake off the realisation of what Jakob had just said. Maybe there was such a thing as being too honest, after all.

She'd heard that term used back at the club too. Hordes. What did the vampires mean by that? She wanted to ask him, but was actually scared to hear his answer. Whatever a horde was, it couldn't be good. She guessed it had to be a group of vampires that weren't as refined as the likes of Marcus, but perhaps wilder. Maybe it was a term for collections of bloodthirsty vampires who lacked the sensibilities those others had? Those missing a conscience or a soul that couldn't be trusted to feed out in the human world, so had to be fed scraps from vampires like Camilla?

Wynter had the suspicion she'd just answered her own question. "So she doesn't have any qualms about killing? And what about the laws?" she asked Jakob, hoping she might be wrong.

"She thinks nothing of killing. Most of our kind don't, but there are rules," Jakob told her, leading Wynter down the hallway towards what she could see was a fire door at the end.

She followed, wandering slowly beside him as he continued to chat with her, and was drawn to him once again thanks to his openness and decency. "Contrary to myth and fiction, we do not shy away from sunlight or can be deterred by garlic or crosses. We cannot be killed with wooden stakes or holy water. Our deaths are administered by decapitation or by us being burned alive."

Wynter wrinkled her nose at the gruesome information, but still nodded in understanding. She was getting a lesson she hadn't even realised she'd needed and listened intently as Jakob continued. It was fascinating to hear, and she still wholeheartedly appreciated the way he spoke with such refreshing honesty.

They went through the doorway and, like at the club, Wynter expected to find more corridors there to ensure they couldn't just escape, but was stunned to instead find themselves going straight out into the cool night air. She looked around and discovered that they were outside a service exit of some kind of stately home, and turned back to look up at the huge house in the darkness.

"What is this place?" she asked, impulsively changing the subject.

"Camilla's residence. She lives at the front of the mansion while those such as Lola and myself live at the back. She much prefers the prettier side," he replied with a playful roll of his eyes.

"While you prefer dark and cold?"

"More like practical and private," he corrected with a smile and then led her over to a garage. There, he opened the huge door to reveal a bright blue sports car that was the exact colour of his eyes, not that she'd noticed of course. Wynter grinned and let herself have a moment to appreciate the beautiful piece of machinery. She didn't know much about cars, but she knew this was something special. And expensive—not that creatures like Jakob had to worry about it of course.

"Understated, just like I expected of Mr Practical and Private," she teased as she climbed in the passenger side and buckled up. "Now, take me out for dinner," she added, and then checked her watch and realised that it was almost five-am, "or breakfast. Whatever. Just feed me."

Jakob watched her with a smile and then shook his head, as though surprised by something. Wynter wanted to ask what, but then remembered her promise to herself. She wasn't going to care what other people thought of her any more. She was going to be herself and do what she wanted with her life. Those around her could get on board or get out.

Look after number one—that was the goal.

He sped away and in just a few moments they'd turned out of the private driveway and onto a winding country road.

Jakob drove insanely fast and Wynter held on for dear life as he took the corners at breakneck speed and flew through lights as if he somehow knew they'd always be green.

She hated every second of it. She was not like those girls in the movies where they always seemed to trust their driver and enjoy the fast ride. Nope, she was more the close her eyes and hope for the best kind of girl. Not one for thrill rides in the slightest.

When they finally came to a stop, it was outside a small shopping village set away from the nearby town and regular shopping areas. Wynter just hoped there might be an early-opening coffee shop, or at least an all-night fast food chain there so she could grab something. Anything!

"Will this do?" Jakob asked as they both climbed out and took a look around at the empty parking lot. "I meant it when I said I didn't know where to get food."

As was expected, the shops were closed, but there was a burger-chain restaurant up ahead and Wynter ran for the door in the hope she might be in luck. She wasn't. The damn place didn't open until six-am. She cursed and stepped back, where she collided with Jakob, whom she hadn't realised had been hot on her heels.

He was quick to grab her so she didn't fall, and she heard him take a sniff of her hair.

"Looks like I'm not the only one who's hungry?" she said, turning to face him, and Jakob seemed surprised by her reaction.

"No, I'd never feed from you, Wynter. You're not mine to taste," he replied with an awkward expression. As if he really and truly would never take from her what Marcus so readily did. It was odd, but also a nice thought to have a vampire companion who didn't want to devour her every five seconds.

"Like you said, people seem to like me well enough. I'm starting to see how I can use that to my advantage," she informed him, and then lifted her hand to show him the mobile phone she'd just taken from his jacket pocket while he'd been flummoxed momentarily.

Wynter grinned mischievously and then pouted when she tried to access the phone but was halted by his passcode. "Tell me your code, Jak. I'll pull up the maps and we can actually go in search of somewhere that's open."

Jakob moved over to her in a heartbeat and had his phone back in his grasp without so much as a struggle from her. She wasn't playing games, and so just continued to smile up at him and then looked down at the phone in his hands. "Hurry up, I'm getting hangry," she demanded, and delighted in his puzzled look.

Before he could ask her what that meant she took off for the parking lot and skipped over to his car, perching by the driver's side. "How about I drive?"

Now that really made him laugh. Jakob was still bellowing out sniggers after he'd physically placed her in the car's passenger seat and buckled her in, and then he turned to Wynter, eyeing her with that same thoughtful look.

Again, he seemed surprised by her, and she liked it.

"I've found a food place that's open," he then said, before starting the engine and tearing away with a screech. They turned out of the shopping village and around the corner, and then it was Wynter's turn to laugh as the bright lights of a huge supermarket came into view. It wasn't exactly the greasy spoon or fast-food breakfast she'd thought, but it would do nicely.

She said nothing as he parked up and followed her inside, sticking awkwardly next to her. Wynter figured Jakob had never been to a supermarket before and she enjoyed being the one to take the lead. She took him into the foyer and ordered for him to grab a trolley, which he just about managed after finally figuring out how to pry the metal carts apart.

She smiled to herself as she watched him, and then realisation struck her. She didn't know how long she'd end up being away and so decided she was going to stock up on supplies. Just the human essentials, but necessities nonetheless. And why not. The supermarket was pretty much empty and actually, she enjoyed the simple pleasure of just being free to do some shopping.

With Jakob in tow, she set about grabbing something to eat and also some snacks and basics for her stay at Camilla's mansion. He followed her up and down the aisles with wide eyes and confusion that was so evident Wynter found it endearing. He really had no idea.

Jakob actually seemed quite sweet and while she could tell he wasn't keen on being away too long, he said nothing to hurry her as she browsed the store and made her selections. It was fun. Probably the most fun she'd had in weeks, and by the time she'd hit the checkout, she was smiling from ear to ear.

FIFTEEN

When they were back at the mansion, Jakob carried the bags of shopping in while Wynter munched on some croissants she'd bought from the supermarket bakery. She'd devoured one after leaving the store before they'd even reached the car and had put the rest aside, not wanting to make a mess of Jakob's posh car, but was already hungry again so hadn't delayed once they were back at Camilla's foreboding home.

The pair of them then went back to the room she'd woken up in and Wynter sat down on the bed with a sigh.

"What's wrong?" Jakob asked with a seemingly genuine frown.

She wasn't sure she could tell him, but she was still so lost. Wynter suddenly felt like she didn't know what she wanted, not really. Put her in a room with Marcus and she knew she'd want him. The same would be for if she were with Warren. Neither one of them had really done anything to warrant her affection though and she wondered if she really was just a fool whenever it came to matters of the heart. Different men had done a number on her time and again, and yet she'd still never learned. And even after having convinced herself for years that she'd found the secret to surviving via her icy mind-set, it appeared she was still back to square one.

"All of this," she replied as she ushered around the room with her hand, meaning the situation she'd found herself in on a whole, not just the how and where of the current situation. "And I get the feeling you're not just spending time with me for my sparkling personality. Are you babysitting me?" Wynter asked with a frown.

"No," Jakob replied with a smile, surprising her.

She looked up at his handsome face and knew she was wearing that doe-eyed look of wonder girls often got when peering into men's faces, but didn't care. His chiselled jaw and hardened stare was still intimidating, but when he smiled, Wynter was captivated. She remembered what it felt like to have him hold her, and let herself indulge in her fantasies a little. After all, what harm could it do? She knew it'd never lead anywhere. He was just another vampire, and his kind did not fornicate with humans. That'd been well and truly drummed into her by now.

"But?" she asked him, and knew there was indeed more to it when he bowed his head slightly as though conceding.

"But I am guarding you. I've been asked to make sure you don't misbehave or try to escape."

"Oh. And if I had tried to run earlier at the store?" Wynter said with a determined look at the vampire she knew was not only stronger and faster than her, but also more cunning and clever. There would be no way she could outrun or outsmart him if she tried, but that didn't mean she'd have to like it.

"I would stop you," Jakob answered curtly, as if it were obvious. "I might not like it either, but I know what's best and that's for you to stay with me."

"With you?" she countered, having found his choice of words a little odd.

"Well, I mean you must stay here and if it's me or Lola watching you, then you're better off with me. Camilla does not care for your safety, only that you comply with her wishes. Lola would not be an ally, but a warden. Someone who would merely keep you safe because she had been ordered to," he answered, but Wynter got the feeling he too was bending the truth a little.

"Tell me more about Camilla," she asked, opting to discuss the more important matter at hand—her official captor. "I need to know what I'm dealing with. Does she intend to kill me?"

"Oh, yes," Jakob answered with a jovial smile, but she knew he was telling the truth. "But only if you don't behave. She wants to take you away from Marcus first as punishment."

"What have I done?" she demanded, feeling hard done by.

"Not you," Jakob chided, "him."

"Oh. And how does she plan to do that?"

"Either by making him abhor you, or vice versa. She had hoped for an easy resolution, but your strength has made that somewhat difficult. You remember I told you we don't mind killing humans? Well that was the old way. Times have changed and we're trying not to do so unless absolutely necessary," he explained, but Wynter was still confused.

"How?"

"We outnumber humans two-to-one. Because of this, we cannot kill them without facing the repercussions. Each human should be kept alive as a slave until they're no longer fit for purpose. Camilla has never entertained that idea, so she feeds at clubs like *Slave* and the numerous others Marcus runs, but she also commands an army of vampires she calls hordes. They're kept hungry and caged. The remains of their human minds broken and lost so that only the feral side is left. They are the ultimate hunting machines and were created as a contingency plan should the human race ever discover our existence and rise up against us. They are trained not to drink their fill, but to take a mere sip and pass their prey along so that the others in their pack survive."

"Oh, God," she replied with a gulp, the realisation striking that she had indeed been right to assume the worst about them. "And Marcus wouldn't drink from me if I have been tainted by the bites of others. He told me so before."

She cursed herself for being such a quick study, and clutched at her aching gut.

"Exactly," Jakob replied, "she won't kill you, but she'll make him refuse your vein by having anything from one to a dozen vampire soldiers feast on your blood."

A chill ran down her spine at the thought.

"So it's that or I escape him some other way?"

"Yes. I guess the only other way would either be by merging your soul with another vampire, or becoming pregnant with another human's child. Either would be enough of a change to spare you his affection for long enough to ensure your escape."

The room suddenly started to spin. There was no way she could imagine herself going that far. No fucking way in hell. She'd rather stay with Marcus.

"But I don't want either of those things!" she bellowed. If she let any of the hordes bite her Marcus wouldn't just turn her away, he'd throw her to the wolves with all his other slaves. She'd have to work in that club feeding them in whatever depraved method he chose. He still wouldn't just let her go free. Nothing was ever that simple when it came to him.

And if she merged with another vampire, then surely that meant they'd have to love one another first? She couldn't give her soul to someone and become their willing slave, because she knew that was what would happen once she merged. There was no doubt her mind and body would no longer be her own. Not really different to her current predicament.

And then there was the third option. Marcella was doing it, she knew, but she couldn't bear to do the same. The idea of bringing a baby into the awful world she'd found herself in was deplorable. She couldn't imagine anything worse.

None of these plans would do. Not a single one.

Wynter decided she would fight tooth and nail with any man, woman, witch or vampire who tried to make her do any of them. This was no longer about just escaping Marcus, but instead this was about her survival in general. She was up against threats from numerous sources, and knew it was time she put her newest plan into place.

She would put herself first like she'd promised and not cave again.

Not even for a second.

Because now, her life well and truly depended on it...

SIXTEEN

"I shan't discuss this with you again, Camilla," Marcus snapped before letting out an exasperated groan. How had he been so blind for all these long years? The damn woman was actually in love with him and yet he'd not seen it before. Not realised the extent of her attraction to him, while he'd taken their liaisons as casual rather than see how she adored him both in and out of the bedroom.

Camilla had indeed played a perilous game in order to get him to her home, and Marcus was livid that it'd worked. She'd moved her pieces into place while he'd been too distracted to see it, and now there he was, her captive. And Wynter too. She was in the belly of the house and was being held there while he played his part of the game. Marcus could sense her, but knew she was well though. Not currently harmed or under any duress. He knew his actions might alter that however, and so treaded carefully whilst dealing with his hostess.

"Then send the girl away, Marcus," Camilla demanded, her voice shrill with jealousy. "Be done with her and things can go back to how they were."

He took a step towards her and fixed his icy stare on

the ancient vampire he knew had the upper hand, for now. Marcus approached and Camilla retreated, but not like Wynter did. Not out of fear. No, she was doing it to lure him towards the bed she'd made up especially for him. She wanted him to take her atop it. To make love to her and have her believe that everything was going to be all right. But he couldn't bring himself to want her or desire the same body he'd been with countless times before. Things had changed.

Her actions had only cemented things for him. He wanted Wynter. He wanted to complete what he'd started a few weeks before and make her his. It was clearer than ever before and Marcus couldn't believe it'd taken him so long to finally see it.

In many ways, he couldn't believe he'd wasted the time playing games and toying with her. She was the only thing on his mind and he was sure now that he was ready to take the next step. He was ready to merge his soul with hers. He had Camilla to thank for pushing him, at least.

"I will not send Wynter away," he groaned honestly, the consequences be damned. He would lie and fight his way out of whatever Camilla threw at him, but he couldn't agree to anything that would damn his darling girl to whatever fate his vampire lover had in store for her.

Marcus knew what had to be done. That he would need to offer Camilla something in exchange for his precious prize, and knew exactly what was needed of him. He had to agree to one more tryst. When it was done, he would take Wynter home and complete the merging process, but he had to do this one thing before he could take her and go.

To save Wynter he had to lie. "I won't send her away because she means nothing more to me than my fondness for the blood running through her veins," he replied with a sour expression.

Camilla seemed surprised, but convinced, and so Marcus moved closer still, giving his ruse everything he had to make it seem real. To make her believe it. "You've let your jealousy get the better of you, my darling. But your fears are unfounded. Here, let me show you. Let me love you…"

And he did.

***

After two days of being stuck under the watchful eye of the strange Russian vampire, Wynter began to see their world in a whole new light. He told her many things as they passed the time together. About the history of his kind and just how many countries were pretty much ruled by them. Jakob talked for hours about the places he'd seen and the people he'd encountered, but he always seemed to hold something back. She wasn't sure why he insisted on it, but Wynter knew she was finally ready to know the truth. She wanted to get the whole story.

"What are you hiding?" she asked as she propped herself up against her pillows and relaxed against them, feeling tired. The days and nights had blurred together in their small room and while she'd had decent amounts of sleep, she hadn't ever slept for long at a time. Not with her guard always watching. Always seeming to be scrutinising her in ways she couldn't fathom. "Your stories, they always end abruptly, like you aren't telling me the whole tale."

Jakob shifted in his seat, seeming uncomfortable for the first time since she'd met him. That just made her more eager to get to the bottom of his unease.

"It's because with me, everything ends badly."

Well, that didn't make any sense. Wynter sat up higher and scratched at the nape of her neck where a chill had just swept over her that seemed to somehow be emanating from Jakob. It was the same when Marcus was in one of his violent rages, and yet Jakob still seemed at ease. Far from the fear-inducing iciness she felt around her master when she'd said or done the wrong thing.

"As in?" she asked in the hope he'd elaborate.

"Death," he eventually groaned, staring blankly through her. "I am known by many as an assassin. A butcher. A fiend," Jakob revealed with a frown, "the village outside Paris I told you about—I burned it to the ground and killed everyone after my visit there. Man, woman and child," he explained, knocking the wind out of her. "If you were to ask me what my trade is, I would answer that I am a reaper. I take those that are living and render them otherwise for hire, or for my own means."

"So all the places you've visited and the people you've known, they were all for jobs? You were there to murder someone?" Wynter asked, her heart pounding in her ears as fear suddenly reared its ugly head and wracked through her. Was that his current job as well? To end her life when he got the call from his mistress?

Jakob nodded, and he didn't even seem sorry.

"For Camilla, but sometimes for others who pay me well. Other times for myself, or perhaps professional curiosity," he said, as though reeling off a simple list of reasons, but Wynter was dismayed.

"Why?" she whispered, her eyes wide. She couldn't imagine taking another person's life, much less if she had to do it without any other reason than because someone was paying her to. It didn't make sense to her at all.

"Why what?" he dared ask, and Wynter shook her head.

"Why her? Why not say no? Why take those lives?"

"Camilla is my sire, Wynter. Vampires hold their sires in the highest esteem and above all others. We serve them and follow in their footsteps, just like any other mentor."

"And if she told you to kill me?" she demanded.

She climbed up out of bed and stood watching Jakob for his answer, her hands on her hips defiantly. "Would you do it without question? Would you even care for the life you'd just snubbed out? Would it matter that we became friends?"

"Yes," he answered, but Wynter didn't know which of her questions he'd meant it for. Either way, she wasn't waiting around here to die. What a cruel game, leaving her locked away, sitting and having nice long chats with the man just waiting for the go-ahead to end her miserable life. She wanted out of there and wasn't going to play nice any longer.

"Screw you," she croaked, and then pulled on her boots and jacket. "And fuck her. I'm not staying here to die."

Wynter stormed out and was surprised when Jakob didn't stop her. She made it all the way to the door at the end of the hallway before he appeared in front of her like some kind of goddamn ghost and scared the crap out of her. Damn them and their ability to move like that.

He stared into her eyes with that all-knowing look again and then Wynter saw him flinch, as if he'd caught a scent from somewhere. She presumed her, but then his eyes darted behind her.

"No, 'dis way," he said, directing her back to the other end of the hallway. "We go 'dis way."

"Why?" she snapped, but Jakob didn't answer. He just took her by the wrist and led her away.

Wynter had no choice but to follow, and had to pick up the pace as Jakob took her down and then through a door at the opposite end of the hallway.

Once inside, he turned to her and put his forefinger to his lips.

"Stay absolutely silent," he told her and Wynter

nodded.

She then looked around and realised they were now inside the main part of the house. Camilla's home.

He then led her deeper into the dark mansion and even though none of the lights were on, Wynter could still see that the foyer they were in was lavishly decorated and filled with ornate marble figures the size of behemoths. As they neared them, she saw they were depictions of roman gods and goddesses. Mythology personified in the artist's own way. She actually quite liked them.

Wynter spied what she assumed had to be the front door and made to go to it, but Jakob appeared to have other ideas. He instead led her up a set of wide stairs to where the only small sliver of light emanated from.

The pair of them then came to a stop outside the door that had been closed but not shut completely. A few inches of space remained, and through it Wynter could see two people thrusting and writhing against each other atop what looked like a huge chaise. She knew right away who the male of the two was. Marcus. He was slamming himself inside the woman beneath him, eliciting cries and groans of delight with every plunge. His suitor was transfixed on him, and she was clearly eager for more.

Wynter stood there frozen. She was glued to the scene before her and knew she ought to look away. Or to give them some privacy at least, but she couldn't. She knew she should be embarrassed, but oddly wasn't.

No, she then realised, she ought to be furious with him for having led her on so much the past few weeks and then coming here to fuck Camilla while she'd had Wynter locked away under the watchful eye of her personal assassin.

But actually, she felt nothing. Not jealous. Not angry. Not even hurt.

The scene before her just proved Jakob right from

before. Marcus didn't love her and never would, but she no longer had to wonder how he felt about her.

She watched him and felt the shutters go down on any feelings she might've once thought she had for him. Wynter knew for sure now how it was all nonsense, every last kiss and fake bit of closeness they'd shared, and all the times he'd let those eyes of his shine brightly.

She meant nothing more than a slave to him and that was fine. It would also make her decision to step away from both him and Warren all that much easier to stick to.

Camilla's cries bought Wynter back to the view before her and she watched as the stunning woman then wrapped her hands around Marcus's neck and squeezed. She grinned as he took the exchange as a challenge and mirrored the move as he continued pounding into her, and then Camilla let out an almighty scream as what had to be an orgasm ripped through her. It was the hottest thing Wynter had ever seen. In spite of her coldness, a raw wave of emotion flooded through her and she didn't try and stop it.

Heat bloomed between her thighs and radiated to her stomach and up her chest. Wynter felt horny as hell and found herself leaning back against the vampire standing pressed right against her. Jakob responded the opposite way Marcus would. Rather than push her away in distaste, he took a deep lungful of her scent and she could tell he liked it when he tilted down his head, buried it in her hair, and took another.

Marcus continued inside the bedroom. He didn't stop and Camilla didn't seem to want him to, and so the pair of them carried on, just as they had been when she and Jakob had found them. And Wynter wanted to watch some more. She put her hand up to her lips and instinctively thought of the times Marcus had kissed her hard the way he was kissing Camilla. And of how he'd touched her and made her climax so very many times now, just like he was with her.

The memory of how his fingers had brought her such pleasure just days before invaded her thoughts and Wynter was soon filled with even more desire.

Marcus's head lifted and she knew he must've caught her scent, but didn't care. Part of her wanted him to find them there, watching him and Camilla fuck. She wanted to be caught while catching him in the act. Wanted to dare him to tell her off, when it was he who had closed those doors by giving into Camilla's desires.

She arched her back against Jakob's torso again, and pushed herself into his tight body. It was wanton and sordid, but she didn't care. In that moment, she needed to feel something. Was desperate for someone to touch her and elicit those climaxes Marcus was drawing from Camilla. Jakob responded by pressing his rock-hard erection against her back before inhaling her scent again, and his hands grabbed her hips, pulling her tighter against him.

Without thinking about what she was doing, Wynter then opened her mouth and emitted the smallest of gasps. The second it left her lips though, the moment was over. Jakob shut down and backed off. He then wrenched her away and spirited her down the stairs so quick she couldn't even think about fighting him back.

Before she knew it they were outside in the cool night air and Jakob was throwing her into the passenger seat of his car. He then sped away without another word and Wynter turned to watch him drive with a teasing smile playing on her lips.

"Let me guess, you thought you'd break my heart by showing me Marcus in the throes of passion with your boss?" she demanded, and got no answer. "Perhaps you weren't counting on me not giving a fuck, hey? Or on me finding the show pretty damn watchable."

Jakob continued to drive in silence and yet Wynter could sense how he was struggling to maintain his composure. He was driving like a maniac and taking the turns even faster than the last time he'd taken her out, but she wasn't exactly calm either and still wanted to say her bit. "Or maybe you're angry that you wanted a piece of what I was so willing to offer you? It's okay if you do, Jak. I'm not afraid to tell the truth about wanting you. No strings. No complications. All you have to do is take it."

Jakob tore the car off the road and drove up an overgrown side road before finally screeching to a halt at the peak of a hill overlooking the mountainous view ahead. Wynter even thought how it would've been a lovely sight in other circumstances, but not necessarily tonight. Not with the predator sat seething beside her.

Once he'd turned off the engine, he was out of the car and on her side in a heartbeat, and all still without a word. At least he'd seemed to calm down, but Wynter was still hesitant as she accepted his hand and let the silent vampire pull her from the car and lead her around to the front of the bonnet before coming to a stop at the grill.

He was brooding, she could tell, and so stared out at the view while letting him make up his mind regarding what he wanted to about what she'd said. After all, she'd been rather candid, and a little vulgar. Wynter felt she'd said more than enough. Done more than enough. Jak had to be convinced by now that she had no real personal tie to Marcus. That she'd meant it when she'd told him she was with him by force and nothing more.

She still wanted a way out, but she wanted an easy way. Not to be rendered disgusting by a horde of vampire soldiers each taking a sip, and not to be sold off to another vampire to become their soul mate. She might as well just stay with Marcus if that were the case.

She closed her eyes and pictured him and Camilla together. She was beautiful in that iconic vintage way Wynter herself loved, and she was envious of her curves and the ample breasts she'd caught sight of in that room. They made a stunning couple.

"You've called me Jak twice now, Wynter," Jakob finally muttered and she opened her eyes to look at him. He was staring out at the world around them and his features were soft, making him look young and almost innocent. "It makes me think of things I shouldn't. Remember a time when I wasn't a vampire. When Camilla wasn't the only mother I knew."

Now that had come as a shock. She hadn't expected him to be reeling from such an innocent nicknaming, but figured it had to remind Jakob of a very different life he must've once led.

"I can stop," she offered. They had developed a rapport over the past few days. Perhaps even a friendship. The last thing Wynter wanted was to make Jakob feel uncomfortable, but at the same time she wanted to know more about what he remembered of his human life. She hoped he wasn't about to take her up on the offer and turned to look at him.

He was bathed in moonlight and was beautiful. God, Wynter wanted him even more. In her quest to begin to love herself, she had also found someone whom she was starting to feel something for. Something worth grasping hold of, rather than push away.

"No," he whispered, "don't."

"Then talk to me, Jak," she replied, "tell me what you want."

His breath hitched and then he was on her.

Jakob had Wynter up on the bonnet of his car with her legs spread and him nestled between them in an instant. He forced his lips on hers and his body was soon pressing against hers like before, his raging boner pushing against her core.

"You were right," he eventually groaned, "I do want you and was shocked by how you responded. But I liked it. I like you. You're a fighter, Wynter. You're strong."

His words reminded her of the same things Marcus had told her, and she grinned at him.

That was much nicer to hear than the things he'd told her before.

"So, is there a way around the merging? Can you take me without the consequences?" she asked, reaching down his body so she could grab his hard-on from outside his jeans. It really was huge and Wynter wanted to see it. To feel it. She was a wanton fiend and couldn't bring herself to care one little bit.

Jakob hissed and pushed himself into her palm, licking his lips. He then grinned and fixed his deep blue eyes on hers.

"Oh, don't worry," he said as he began stripping her with haste, "you can't merge if you have no soul, Wynter." He then laid her back and unbuttoned her jeans, sliding them down before pulling them off along with her underwear, leaving her naked atop the car before him.

The winter air pricked her skin but she didn't care. She was so hot. Too hot. All she wanted was for Jak to make it better, and as he kissed his way up her thighs and then to her core, she was delighted to discover he wanted to help her too.

Wynter cried out as his tongue delved inside of her and then swirled up and around her clit in perfect motions. She soon came for him and then could do nothing but stare in awe as he then removed his clothes and mounted her atop the car.

Every inch he pushed inside was like heaven, and she cried out as he took her body and made it whole at last.

Jakob was truly a stunning and virile man. More beautiful than any sunrise or sunset, and even better than the bright and very full moon that shone overhead as he pushed into her over and over. She was mesmerised by the stunning view, and lapped it up as he continued to take what she so willingly offered.

SEVENTEEN

Jakob was wild and rough with her atop that car bonnet, and Wynter loved every second of it. He took her every which way she could imagine on one surface and they both came over and over again. Sometimes together, and other times to their own rhythm, but every one somehow seemed more powerful than the last.

It was like nothing she'd experienced before. The power as he commanded her body was astounding, and the stamina? She thought he might never tire.

He threw her across the car bonnet on her stomach and was inside her again a second later, his hands fisted in her long mess of hair. Jakob then yanked her head up and back, arching her against him.

"Jak!" she cried, "please…"

He shushed her and yanked harder, her scalp burning with the pain.

"Stop that," he growled, "you're nothing, do you hear me? Nothing but an empty shell. You don't feel pain…"

She wanted to scream at him. To tell him off. But at the same time, she couldn't deny that it was true. There was an empty void within her that she slowly understood needed filling, and by being with him it was just the beginning. The start of her selfish quest to find herself again.

She didn't need to beg or plead with him to give her what she needed either. He was giving her what she wanted freely and so it was up to her to take it. To use him and fulfil her needs.

And so she did.

They only stopped when a light rain started to fall, making her finally shudder and begin to feel the cold. Jakob was attentive to her response to the elements and so lifted her into his arms and took her to the backseat, where he warmed her with his body before fucking her some more. He didn't seem ready to stop, and while she was beginning to tire, she wasn't ready either.

His mouth was back on her and never left. Either on her lips or breasts, and sometimes her neck and shoulders as he kissed and nibbled at her, but he never once drew blood. He was more dominant and predatory than bloodthirsty, and Wynter trusted him not to take that which Marcus thought nothing of drawing from her time and time again.

Jakob wasn't gentle though. He wrenched on her hair with his fingers some more and commanded her by force, and not once did Wynter stop him, because she wanted it too. She loved being owned. Being taken. It'd been far too long and she'd missed being fucked raw by an expert lover. Not a single one from her past compared to the vampire between her legs and even when her energy waned, she refused to stop because it was exactly what she'd needed.

"Jak," she whispered against him, "don't stop, please."

"Don't beg. Don't plead," he reminded her, and she nodded. "Who do you love?" he then groaned, watching her with hooded eyes and a dark smile.

"No one," Wynter hissed, and then she cried out

when his hand shot around her neck and yanked her hard against him. He was such a brute, and she adored it. "No one but myself," she then whimpered, and let out a satisfied sigh when he came deep within her and then removed his hand.

"Too fucking right," he croaked before kissing her again. But this time, he didn't keep going like before. Jakob began to slow his movements, and she had a feeling this was it. Their night together was finishing up at last.

Wynter didn't want their affair to be over yet though, because she had a sneaking suspicion that when it was, she'd have to go back to that room in the mansion and act like nothing had happened. To go along with whatever plan that witch Lola had in store for her, or worse, Camilla.

When the sun began to creep over the horizon, Jakob let her come one last time and then slowed even more, and he then began to touch her with surprising gentleness. He'd been such a heavy-handed lover that Wynter had wondered if he'd forgotten how, but then his hands suddenly roved her body in tender sweeps and his plunges were deep and delicate, rather than hard and fast.

"Well, what a surprise you are Mr Big Bad Assassin," she teased, "I wouldn't be amazed if you could carry on for days."

"When the mood takes us, vampires can indeed go for days. It's you humans that cannot keep up," he replied with a smile, and then kissed her tenderly.

He then mumbled something she couldn't understand and when he looked into her eyes, Wynter that knew what Jakob had said wasn't for her, but for himself. He'd spoken in Russian instead of English and rather than fret, she smiled.

"Whatever it is, you don't need to worry, Jak," she whispered against him, "I told you. No strings."

He shook his head and whispered the same phrase again and this time, and Wynter frowned at him questioningly.

"It's nothing. Let's go," he grumbled, lifting her up. Rather than push him to tell her the truth, she just followed his lead without argument. She didn't want to end their night with a fight, so figured it'd be easier to relax and leave him be.

She pulled on her dirty clothes and then climbed back into the passenger seat, where she turned to watch him drive. Jakob was closed-off again but he seemed relaxed enough and she smiled, thinking of their amazing night together. She hoped they'd be able to do it again sometime soon. "Here," he suddenly said as he turned to her with a boyish smile, and then lifted the centre armrest to reveal a small compartment. Inside were a dozen cereal bars and a couple of bottles of mineral water. "I remembered to feed you this time," Jakob added with a small laugh, which Wynter echoed.

She thanked him and helped herself, watching out the windscreen as he drove them away in what was now a heavy, thundering rain.

He was slow this time though. Leisurely. Like he didn't want to rush back, and Wynter smiled to herself as she took another bite of her makeshift meal.

When she was finished, she shifted in her seat and peered out at the grey and wet morning, but didn't care. Nothing was going to dampen her mood. They'd had a night to remember and she didn't regret a thing. If anything, it'd been exactly what she'd needed and the perfect way to re-establish her new mantra. She'd done exactly as she'd wanted to do. Taken charge of her self and her future, and had gone onto have the night of her life. And why the hell not? She was beholden to no one and had let her impulses lead her. No harm had been done and she felt amazing.

Tiredness claimed her after eating and relaxing in the

warmth of the heated seat, and soon Wynter was dropping off to sleep. She tried to stop herself, but it was no use. Her body had been thoroughly worked out and now it was time to rest. She let out a soft moan and then felt a hand on her thigh. It was a gentle, reassuring hold, and she liked it. "Sleep now, Wynter," Jakob then told her, "we have a long drive ahead of us."

"Huh?" she grumbled with a frown, wondering why they weren't heading back to the mansion. He didn't give her an answer, and actually, she didn't really care, so she just put her trust in him and let herself succumb to her body's need for rest.

•

When she awoke, it was late morning and they were still on the motorway heading south. The rain had stopped and a bright winter's day seemed to lie ahead, and she stretched as best she could in her seat. Wynter hadn't slept particularly well, but she felt good, in spite of her having had just a few hours' brought on by sheer exhaustion, and didn't mind the warmth still resonating from between her thighs. The memory of her and Jakob's night together was so fresh she wanted to blush, but instead she just grinned to herself and took a few gulps of water from the bottle beside her. There was no doubt about it, their time together had been amazing, and she wasn't going to let anything make her feel bad for having let him take her over and over again both atop and inside of the same car they were still travelling in.

She then caught Jakob watching her with a soft smile and couldn't get over how much she was beginning to like that damn face of his. And his company. She didn't crave space like she did with Marcus after their liaisons were over, and while it scared her to think of how much trouble those emotions could get her into, she also reminded herself of how she'd promised not to shy away anymore. Not to close herself off from her feelings.

Nope, she was embracing them. Becoming a whole person again, not just an empty shell. So, she remained strong and attempted to be fearless in the face of her desires. Yeah, she liked Jak and wanted to be around him some more. Big deal. It didn't mean that anything between them was forever. Even if it was just for a few more days, that'd do nicely.

"How much longer?" she asked, her bladder having given her a sure signal that it needed addressing soon.

"We're almost there," he answered, and soon pulled off the motorway and down towards the coast. He was right, and it wasn't long until he'd pulled up at a tall red brick house that overlooked the ocean via some rocky cliffs with a beach further below them. The cool sunshine was beaming down on them, lighting up the epic stretch of coast brightly, and Wynter soaked up the view.

Jak then cut the engine and they sat there in silence for a moment. The wind seemed to be picking up outside, but there was still some lingering warmth, and she stared out at the scenery with a smile. It was truly stunning, and Wynter stopped and let herself admire it before she climbed out of the car with another stretch, but Jakob seemed intent on getting her inside rather than linger to take in the sights any longer. He hurried her along, and she decided against arguing so headed inside behind her immortal companion without delay.

The interior of the quaint home was not a let down. She was pleased to discover it had been not only cleaned and fully furnished ready for their stay, but also seemed to be fully equipped with necessities and essentials, plus the food supplies had thankfully been well stocked by the looks of things. She had a quick look around, but soon followed Jak upstairs to a huge master bedroom rather than stay downstairs alone.

Wynter then watched him check every inch of the place, as if he was looking for bugs or something. Jakob even ran his hands over each of the windows and made sure their locks were secure. He clearly didn't want any unannounced visitors.

"What is this place?" she eventually asked, and then took a seat on the huge king sized bed. There were clothes in a small pile atop the duvet, and Wynter picked them up and started to check each one out while she waited for Jakob to answer her. They were all her size. Someone had clearly been expecting her.

"Safe," was all he replied, but it was enough. A word that held many meanings of course, but she trusted in his knowledge and expertise. And in his wisdom and guidance. If Jakob had brought her here to keep her safe, then she'd stay, and so she headed for the bathroom without argument and with a contented smile on her still tired face.

It was so odd how comfortable she felt with him though. She even wondered if she was under some kind of new spell? But surely not. Jak wasn't the sort to do that to her.

Maybe she was just happy? Or whatever semblance of it she was capable of while still knowing what chaos laid ahead. Wynter couldn't deny feeling pleased with the erotic turn of events the night before. It had been nice to get away from the scrutiny and vile company Marcus often was. It was even good to get away from the club for a few nights, and even though things could go sour in a heartbeat, she didn't care. For now, she'd just settle for the happy little bubble she'd found herself in.

She used the facilities, brushed her teeth, and then took a long and hot shower. It felt amazing to get freshened up and when she emerged, she felt good as new as she finished drying off and slid into a pair of pyjamas she'd found among the new clothing that'd awaited her arrival.

Jakob was waiting for her, evidently having finished

his checks. He too had washed up somewhere, and when she clambered into bed, he climbed in behind her, spooning around her while stroking her freshly washed skin.

Damn, that felt so good. He was warm and tender, and even though she knew she was in the company of a killer, she had never felt safer.

Wynter began to arch against him on instinct. How could she want him again so soon? But there it was, that flourish of heat blooming between them. The need that was building again.

He kissed and caressed her neck, whispering foreign words while enticing her body with his touch. Wynter didn't ask his reasons why, but knew he wanted her again too, and so she turned her body towards his and peered up into his impossibly deep blue eyes. They were a whole different colour to Marcus's. His were icy, while Jakob's were warm. Like the colour of sapphires.

"What is that you keep saying, Jak?" she had to ask, and was disheartened when he frowned, like he didn't want to tell. But then he sighed and pulled her closer.

"I keep saying to myself, and to you, that it'll be okay. I won't have to do it. There will be another choice," he answered, but Wynter barely felt any clearer.

"Do what?" she had to ask.

Jakob shuffled and looked away as if he were ashamed to say it, but Wynter put her hand on his cheek and pulled him back, locking their gazes again.

"Kill you," he then croaked, and she finally understood his unease. They really were in a lot of trouble, she realised.

"But if she says to, you'll do it without hesitation?"

He didn't want to say it, she could tell, but Wynter needed to hear him with her own ears. She had to know, and still wasn't scared. Foolish or not, she continued to have hope that things would work out somehow.

In fact, there was also a part of her preferred death

as a way out. She didn't want to face any of Lola's offered alternatives other than being free to walk away unscathed, and the thought of dying when compared to either being turned, bitten, impregnated, or merged with someone she couldn't possibly love, didn't seem quite so bad.

"Yes," he confirmed with a pained expression, "you have no idea what it's like, Wynter. She's my sire and that bond can never be broken. Not until—"

"I don't want to hear your reasons why, Jak," she told him calmly, and still smiled. "If I have to die then how better than by your hand? So no more fretting over it, okay?"

Jakob stared down at her in wonder and then shook his head.

"You are a miracle to me," he told Wynter as he climbed over her, pulled off her clothes, and then positioned himself between her thighs. "One I shall admire long after our time together is over."

Wynter took the strange compliment as she hoped he'd intended it, and then readied herself for another round of his fierce fucking, but instead Jakob continued with his gentle, leisurely pace from before. He slid inside and nestled himself there, looking down at her admiringly as he took her, and Wynter basked in his adoration.

It was sheer heaven. No one had ever been so attentive with her before. So loving and caring.

I could die right now and go happily, she then thought as he made love to her.

Even as the night fell later that evening, Wynter and Jakob continued their exploits in the bedroom and only let up when the incessant ringing of his mobile phone was just too hard to ignore any longer.

She headed for the bathroom while he took the call, and Wynter could hear him barking down the phone in

Russian to whoever was on the other end. She presumed either Lola or Camilla, and was actually glad to be out of the conversation as she had the feeling she might not like what was being said between them. Presumably something vile about her.

She then diverted for the kitchen rather than nestle back under the sheets and was stood perusing the contents of the fridge when Jakob came down to join her.

"Who stocked up for me?" she asked, her head still in the huge door of the appliance. There was a bit of everything and some real thought had gone into it. Human thought. "And the clothes?"

"I have contacts," Jakob answered, and then he went quiet for a second as he watched her. "This house is cloaked by magic and is a kind of safe house for those who need some space from the elders of any kind. Vampires cannot enter without permission and witches are completely unable to find it. A group of rebel humans use rune magic to create barriers like this and they were the ones I contacted to give us some sanctuary for a while. I told them your clothes size and that you like to eat."

Wynter let out a laugh. Well, that was an overstatement. She needed to eat, there was a difference.

"And now that they've finished fucking, I'm guessing Marcus and Camilla want to know where we are?" she mused, plucking some ham and cheese from the shelf and a couple of eggs. Wynter then began chopping the meat and she grated an edge of the yellow block, her focus on her task rather than on Jakob. She wasn't sure she could deal with too much dark and depressive right now. Not after the amazing couple of days together they'd just had. All she wanted was for time to stand still and for everyone to leave them alone. Let them have their time together. Let them be happy, even if just for a short while.

"I told them we went for a drive," he replied, watching her intently. "You're under my watchful eye now, Wynter. Camilla knows I wouldn't let you out of my sight and she is satisfied—for now."

"And Marcus?" she asked as she whisked the eggs in a bowl and threw them in a hot pan with the fillings.

"He's furious," Jakob answered with a smirk.

"Understandably."

"He demanded that I return you forthwith," he said with a confused expression. "Such strange words he uses."

Wynter laughed and finally gave Jakob her full attention. He was beyond cute, but it was obvious he was holding something back.

"Or else?" she guessed.

"He has nothing he can threaten me with," Jakob replied, but Wynter wasn't happy. She flipped her omelette over and then stared into the flames beneath the pan while the other side cooked.

"But I do," she hissed, "does he know I went with you by choice? Does he know we're hiding away so we can have a dirty weekend without him knowing?"

"No," Jakob told her, "I was sure to let Camilla think I did this for the purely tactical advantages, when instead I did it for my personal reasons."

"So you lied? I didn't think you ever lied, Jak?" Wynter countered as she shut off the gas and then transferred the omelette to a plate. But all of a sudden, she was no longer hungry.

She was afraid instead. Part of her wanted to demand they jump in his car and go back. She would appease Marcus in whatever way he demanded and go with him. Leave all of this behind—including her hopes that something might actually change. She couldn't risk the lives of those she cared about.

"I didn't lie, but I told part truths. I gave Camilla only what she needed, and not the full story."

Jakob then crossed the room and pulled Wynter to him. He smoothed her messy hair away from her face and watched her with his brows tightly knit in a frown. "But do not fret, Wynter. This is what she wants. You're out of the way and she can have Marcus to herself, and she will keep him busy. This is the best alternative for now."

"Until he resists her advances and she takes her jealousy out on me again," she replied sourly, and wanted nothing more than for Jakob to shake his head and tell her she was being foolish. But of course, he didn't. She was right.

"That's why we're here," he assured her, "so she cannot make either of us do anything we don't want to. I took you far away from the mansion so that she cannot act against you without first having a clearer head. And also so he cannot come charging in after you and prove her right."

Jakob then planted a soft kiss against Wynter's lips and smiled. "And so I can have you all to myself a while longer," he added, before pushing her still untouched food towards her, "now, eat."

***

Marcus was livid. After everything he had forced himself to do in that bedroom with Camilla he still didn't have Wynter back by his side like she ought to be. Jakob had taken her away and not told a soul where the pair of them were, and Marcus believed Camilla when she said she had no clue where they might be. It was just like the devious assassin to steal his precious slave away and hide her. And just like his mistress to have ordered him to do it.

He'd better not have dared taste her blood. Marcus seethed with just the thought of Wynter being tainted by his bite and could do nothing but pace the bedroom in wait for Camilla to reappear. She'd of course offered for him to go home to the club and return to his other managers. She'd insisted she would send word when Jakob and Wynter were back, but that was not an option. He had instead told Camilla he'd wait with her a while longer.

If he left now there would be nothing but a battle on his hands to get Wynter back. Camilla would feed him excuse after excuse and Jakob would be the same. They were playing him for a fool and he wanted nothing more than to teach them both exactly who they were dealing with.

He needed a plan. A strategy.

His Priestess was the only one who could be trusted to give it to him. But she couldn't come into the mansion or else face the wrath of Camilla for trespassing on another witch's territory, and he couldn't have that. There was nothing else to be done but for him to act on this treachery alone.

He could wait it out and be patient, but instead, he wanted to give Camilla a reason to hate him. For her to see that she couldn't control him no matter what she tried. Perhaps he'd set fire to everything she had built and make her watch it burn, just because he could.

In search of inspiration, he headed out of the bedroom and straight for the nearest set of stairs, where he caught the lingering scent of his darling Wynter. She had been here, in this part of the house. She hadn't been alone either, nor had she been afraid.

Marcus took a deep drag of the scent and cursed. Wynter had indeed been here, and she'd been horny as hell while she was at it. He could taste her pheromones on the air.

Had she seen him in the throes of passion with Camilla? Yes, she had to have witnessed the pair of them. And he knew exactly which vampire had led her to them. The Russian. Someone else who would now have to die simply because Marcus desired it so. How dare he bring Wynter up to watch them? What had he hoped to gain by it? Her compliance and disgust? But his plan hadn't worked. Jakob had hoped the sight would repulse her, but instead she'd been stirred up into a sexual frenzy by what she'd seen. She had enjoyed the view.

Marcus smiled to himself at the thought. Oh, how the tables had turned. His darling had watched him fuck another vampire and the fire she had for him had only been fanned, rather than put out. Had she enjoyed seeing him naked and going for it with Camilla? Had she wanted to touch herself because of it? Or perhaps yearned to be touched by the same vampire she had ran both from and towards these past few weeks?

Yes, he was sure she had, and damn if that didn't make him want her back all the more.

He was out the front door and around the side of the huge building in a heartbeat, where he stood and took stock of the situation at hand.

Camilla had spirited Wynter away and lured him to her bed, willing or not. Her chief minion had then taken steps to move his slave while they were too busy to notice them leave, and now she was gone and Marcus knew he wouldn't rest until she'd come back to him.

As he stared out across the huge areas of land around Camilla's stately mansion, a plan began to form in his mind. There were a dozen or so underground bunkers lying head of him under the ground. They were shelters created for one purpose alone, to hide their contents. They were not a place to seek shelter should the threat of nuclear attack come, or a safe house for the slaves and their masters come the end of days, but quite the opposite. They were created to keep its occupants locked inside. Sealed away. Of course, they were the holding facilities for Camilla's hordes.

He sniffed out the group of most emaciated

vampires from the collection of bunkers and approached the only entrance, a cover that was set in the ground above their nest. It was little more than a manhole, and he lifted it aside without any exertion at all.

Marcus then looked down into the hole and spied the fifty pairs of shining red eyes looking back up at him. To anyone else it might be an eerie sight, but not to him. These men and women would soon become his brothers in arms. His comrades. His newest slaves.

Each of the naked soldiers was clambering closer to the small source of light and—most importantly for them—the prospect of food. They were nothing but wild animals taught and trained through starvation and fear, but today some were going to be freed. They would be enlisted to help him. Do him a service.

Exact his revenge.

Using his teeth, Marcus tore open the vein at his own wrist and then held his arm over the hole. He then watched as his blood cascaded down into the pit, and gave it a few seconds before he healed the wound again and pulled his hand back. The soldiers below scurried to get a coveted taste of the precious life source, and soon he could hear them fighting over the remains.

"What are you doing!" a shrill voice hollered from the house and Marcus turned to the sound with the biggest of grins on his face. He then watched as Camilla's Priestess, Lola, approached at speed. She was clearly terrified of what lay in the pit behind Marcus, and rightly so, but she still ran forwards regardless and he had to stop himself from saying anything that might reveal what he'd just done. She couldn't know until it was too late, for both her and her mistress.

Lola soon reached him and Marcus watched her eyes dart from his mouth to his wrist. She spied the blood he'd spilled and inhaled deeply, ready to scream and warn Camilla what he'd done, but Marcus grabbed his prey and placed his hand over her mouth to silence her.

"Now, now. Don't ruin the fun, little witch," he whispered in her ear before then tossing her down into the pit headfirst.

The scurry of the many for a drink from their solitary sacrificial lamb was audible, but it was of course only a special few who properly took their fill. The strongest and most cunning, and of course those who had already had some blood that fateful morning. His blood.

He listened as they drank Lola dry and then Marcus stood back, watching and waiting for them to act. To seek out their freedom and obey a new master.

The first of the soldiers leapt up and out of the hole mere seconds later, followed by another, and another. When there were five immortal warriors standing before him, each of them covered in blood and lacking of both clothing and hair, or even colour, Marcus nodded and smiled.

He looked at each of them and saw nothing but beasts. Creatures who were now ready and willing to do his bidding thanks to him having fed them his blood. It was an ancient rite that had bound them to one another, and had brought forth a covenant between them all.

Marcus was their master now. Their new sire. The five had been born again thanks to his blood offering, and they would serve him until their last breath. "Welcome, friends. What say we have some fun?" he asked, receiving grunts from each of the huge men in affirmation.

A wide smile spread across his face. This was going to be fun.

He sent them a wordless order to follow him, and the biggest fell directly in line at his right hand side. Marcus looked the alpha of the small pack up and down, watching as he moved with stealth and precision to each and every movement. The man was built like a bodybuilder. He was a behemoth and Marcus was glad he'd absconded from Camilla's reign and joined him instead. This one would make the perfect leader of his unholy army.

Marcus led the handful of soldiers straight over to the mansion, where he pointed to the building and sent them another unspoken, yet clear, order.

Kill them all.

Hunt any stragglers down.

Bring me my darling Wynter, along with Camilla's head.

EIGHTEEN

Jakob's phone wouldn't stop ringing again, but this time it was interrupting Wynter's much needed rest so she kicked him out of bed to go get it. She tried to go back to sleep, but realised the moment he answered it that something was seriously wrong. He was shouting back to someone on the other end and Wynter could hear them screaming down the line at him from where she was still laid feet away.

"*Da*," he finally muttered in a stone-cold tone, and his body language changed entirely. The shutters suddenly went down, and he turned to Wynter who saw him swallow hard.

Something life changing had just happened. Before he even said a word to her, she knew. It was over. Jakob hung up the phone and then physically crumbled onto the bed. She'd never seen him like this before and didn't know what to do, so just tried to comfort him while asking what was wrong.

"Please talk to me, Jak," she implored after repeatedly getting nothing back off him, and eventually he turned his wide blue eyes upwards at her.

"You were right. Marcus has retaliated because of

your disappearance," he croaked. "Camilla got away but she's the only survivor."

"What?" she cried, trying to fathom what that could mean. The only survivor? Out of how many? Jakob stared down at her and he grimaced.

"She's coming here. I have to tell her where we are. I have no choice other than to offer her safety with us."

Wynter leapt to her feet and began pacing. Her heart was pounding in her chest and she knew before he said another thing what to expect when Camilla arrived. The vampire might be coming to seek refuge, but once she had it, it would be the human who was no longer safe.

Camilla would do some retaliating of her own.

"She's your sire," she whispered, a tear rolling down her face. "You protect her and no one else. Obey her alone, no matter what you want for me."

"No," Jakob tried, watching her through hooded eyes, "I'll tell her you're innocent. That you don't deserve to die."

"And then she'll kill us both," Wynter told him with a sad smile. Jakob opened his mouth as though he was about to disagree, but he couldn't. They both knew what was coming for them, and it wasn't going to end up with either getting what they wanted. One would have to concede.

"I'll have to kill you, Wynter. Camilla will force me," he growled and sent a punch flying towards the nearby headboard. "You must run. Now!"

She shook her head no.

"You'd catch me. That or Marcus—"

"Then choose Marcus. At least that way you'll be alive!"

Wynter breathed a deep sigh and clutched her aching belly. Yes, that was a viable alternative, but she wasn't sure she could bring herself to go to him. Not after everything she and Jakob had shared and the decisions she had made to finally start looking after herself. She had a plan now. She was going to become whole and find a way to be free. A way to live her life for her a no one else.

And especially after how amazing things had been between them. Against all odds and them both having told each other it meant nothing, their liaison had indeed ended up meaning everything to her. She had felt free with Jakob and finally knew what it felt like to care again. To see the world without the cloud of hate and iciness looming over her. Wynter cared about so much again. She cared for herself, just like he had told her to, and didn't want Marcus to touch her ever again.

"His eyes glow when we're together," she told Jakob dejectedly, "his soul wants mine and if I go back to him now, we'll merge and then he'll turn me. The Priestess showed me my future before and I wanted to believe I could change it, but now I know for sure that if I go to him, what I saw will come true."

Wynter took a step towards Jakob and climbed to her knees before him. She then turned her gaze up to meet his and let her tears fall. "I don't want that because I want you, Jak. I think... I love you. And, I choose you," she then told him, "only you. Let's run away together."

"He'll never let us go," the shocked vampire answered her, "he'll kill us for trying, but I'm willing to do it if it means we can be together."

"Me too..."

But then Jakob let out a garbled cry and he shook his head furiously. He began scratching at the back of his neck with rough, deep gouges while muttering words in Russian she couldn't understand. Wynter wondered if he was trying to cause himself pain and reached up to stop him. She wrenched his hands away and held them to her cheeks instead.

"She won't let us go either. I will have to kill you," he ground, "I'll have no other choice!"

And there, like a jolt to her chest, was the realisation that she had seen this before. Like some kind of sudden déjà vu, Wynter remembered the vision the Priestess had given her. Of her and the man she wanted instead of Marcus. The life she would try and choose for herself, even if it meant running from the vampire who was clearly not even remotely ready to let her go.

And yet, there was no chance for them. She knew it now, and was sure Jak had known all along.

Wynter decided enough was enough.

"Okay, but I want you to do it. Because who better to take me away from this world full of monsters than you, Jak? When the time comes, I need for it to be you. Promise me…"

As expected, Camilla arrived a few hours' later and Wynter watched as Jakob walked to the edge of the property and invited her inside the magical perimeter. She could see the vampire do a double take, as if she'd seen nothing more than coastline before being given the power to enter the house through the magical warding, and was relieved to see that the spell cloaking them was indeed working.

The pair of them then stopped just inside the boundary and Wynter saw them talking in hushed voices. She wanted to shout and tell them they needn't bother on her account, but bit her tongue. She wasn't after a fight and just hoped Jak could talk some sense into his sire. Plus, Camilla looked in a pretty sorry state. Someone had taken chunks out of her and she was far from the delicate and dainty woman Wynter had spied on just a couple of nights before. She looked a wreck, and as if it'd not been easy getting herself away from whatever had gone down at the mansion.

She continued to watch them from the doorway and bristled when Camilla then suddenly approached her at relative speed. She stormed towards Wynter with a face like thunder and swiftly backhanded her, knocking her flying to the ground.

She screamed in pain with the sting of it, but still turned her face up to glower at Camilla.

"Let me guess, I somehow did something wrong, even though I was miles away?" she seethed, clutching her stinging cheek. "You brought this on yourself by messing with him. Don't try and blame me."

"You do not speak to me, you insolent little bitch," Camilla roared, raising her hand as if to strike her again, but Jakob got between them.

"No," he told her, making Camilla do a double take.

"No?" she demanded, "where do you get off telling me no? Marcus has ruined me, Jakob. My entire life was in that house and now he's taken it from me, along with the hordes. He... he," she started to cry, "he killed Lola and then sent them after me. After everyone at the house. He won't stop until he gets his little whore back so I'm going to personally see to it that he never does."

They all fell silent at her vicious words, each of them waiting to se what the other did like some kind of standoff.

"I take it you want me to kill her?" Jakob eventually asked her coldly, and while she'd told him previously how she wanted it, Wynter hoped it was a front. That he was just figuring out Camilla's game first.

"No, worse," the vampire answered with a sneer, "I want her to suffer like I have suffered. I want her to be broken and abused, violated and so far from the woman he knew that he won't be able to stand the sight of her."

It was Wynter's turn to cry now. This was indeed a fate worse than death. She was starting to wish she'd run when Jakob had given her the chance.

"Then you don't need my services," he told his sire, shocking them both.

He said nothing else on the subject and simply walked into the house as if nothing were awry, leaving the two of them out on the front step glaring back at him in disbelief.

***

Marcus grew closer. He could smell Camilla in the air and as he tracked her, another scent began to invade his senses.

Wynter.

Her arousal had increased and her scent was tangy with the fervour of it. She had been having her share of excitement without him and jealousy flared within him. Was it due to a bite from her captor? For their sakes, he hoped not. But knew he'd find out soon.

They were close. His personal soldiers were hot on Camilla's scent too and together they ran beneath the full moon like proper creatures of the night, covering vast amounts of space with barely an ounce of effort. Just like the stories said, they were predators and would not stop until they caught their prey.

They had each fed well back at the mansion too, even Marcus, and had energy aplenty for the run. And more than enough for the fight that then would lie before them.

The suburban world their group were immersed in was chaotic with many scents and sounds to sort from, but soon opened up to reveal the ocean ahead of them. They had reached the edge of the country and were now running along the coast and for a moment, Marcus wondered if their prey had boarded a vessel and sailed away in a bid to evade him, but no. The scent of the wounded vampire stopped abruptly before a cliff edge. Not a harbour or a dock of some kind.

He moved closer to the edge and tried to pick out the smell of either female he was tracking. Camilla's scent had indeed come to an abrupt stop and then linger on the breeze, whereas Wynter's scent seemed to surround him, but from nowhere distinguishable at all. She was close by but he couldn't pin point her location, like she was there but had somehow been hidden.

He edged closer still and felt that there was more than he could see and feel. Something beyond their reach.

A safe house cloaked in magic. That had to be it. Jakob had enlisted the help of friends in both the human and supernatural worlds to help him hide Wynter, but he hadn't counted on the foolishness of his sire. She hadn't covered her tracks at all and had led them straight to their hideout. It was the only reason he'd let her escape the mansion in one piece after all, but she'd still not seen it. Marcus shook his head. He'd given Camilla far too much credit over the years. It was a wonder they hadn't come to an end sooner.

He then sent a silent order for his soldiers to stand in a semi-circle around the source of Wynter's scent, and then lie in wait. To watch and not take their eyes away. To not leave for even a second. Not until he found a way inside, which was when they were to come in with him and take Camilla down. The others, he told them, were for their master.

He would rip Jakob to pieces and then take his prized possession back where she belonged, and he would merge with her. And when she had turned, they would return to his newly acquired property and rebuild the house and business that Camilla had once owned.

He would make it in his image though, and command the hordes forevermore, but this time, it would be with Wynter by his side.

It was going to be perfect. All he had to do now was ensure the plan worked in his favour.

NINETEEN

Camilla was pacing.

Jakob was brooding.

Wynter was wringing her hands and trying desperately not to stare out the window at the veritable gang of scary as hell vampires standing vigil outside the property. Who were those other five? She'd never seen them before, and couldn't bear to keep looking either. They were like vampire zombies or something. Each of them had pale, greying skin and red eyes. They were each bald and had been dressed in a simple shirt and jeans, but none of them had any shoes on.

They had to be the soldiers Jak had told her about. And if they were standing guard at Marcus's command, then that meant their allegiance had changed. Camilla was no help to her now, especially not after having lost everything to Marcus, whose power was undoubtedly growing.

"What's the point of us staying here if we have no means of escape?" Camilla eventually shrieked and Jakob jumped to his feet and glowered at her.

"Maybe if you'd thought twice about covering your tracks they wouldn't have come within an hour of your arrival!" he spat, and then in a surprise move, came and sat beside Wynter on the sofa. He put his arm around her shoulders and held her close, shushing her sobs and the pair of them tried to relax, but it was no use. Camilla was right, they needed a plan, and fast.

"Just let me go to him. I'll lie and pretend I was here alone," she tried, but Jakob wouldn't hear of it.

"Marcus knows Camilla is here and he knew we were together. He won't believe you're the innocent captive," he reminded her and Wynter nodded. She then looked over her shoulder out to where the six vampires still stood, patiently waiting for their prey to come to them.

"Give me your phone," she told him, and Jakob did as she asked but it was evident by the sour look on his face that he wasn't keen on whatever idea she had in mind.

She dialled Marcus's number, thinking it was a long shot, but that it just might work.

Wynter then climbed up onto the sofa on her knees and faced the window, watching as Marcus reacted to the phone vibrating in his pocket and then plucked it out. He grinned down at it smugly and then answered the call before lifting it to his ear.

"You've given up quicker than I would've expected, Jakob. I'm surprised," his voice echoed down the line and Wynter let out a small cry at how deadly his tone was. How feral. Marcus had come to claim what was his and she knew he'd kill anyone who got in his way. There was no way out of this for Camilla, but she knew she might be able to at least negotiate some kind of a deal for Jakob. After all, he had kept Wynter safe like he'd promised. "My sweet..." Marcus sighed, having heard her and realised it wasn't the phone's owner on the other end. "I've missed you."

"And I you, Marcus," she lied, "have you come to take me home?"

"Indeed I have," he replied, and Wynter watched as

his smile began to widen at hearing her compliance. "Why don't you invite me in and we can be done with this farce?"

"I would, but I have made promises to Camilla and Jakob to secure their safety. She came here to ensure you no longer wanted me, Marcus. To ruin my body and mind as she saw fit, but I have struck a deal. My life for hers. Jakob's too."

"I will not honour any such deal," he ground, and she stared out the window at him, and his face was like thunder.

"Then I cannot leave," she told him, and then peered down at Jakob, who urged her to deepen the threat. He mouthed to her to go on. To make Marcus believe it and act on her warnings. "Jakob has me at his mercy, Marcus. He will kill me and has told me so on more than one occasion. The only way to spare my life is to meet his demands."

"Then it appears we are at an impasse," he replied before abruptly ending the call.

Apparently he wasn't in the mood to negotiate.

Wynter then watched in horror as he walked over to a nearby parked car, lifted it up off the ground with ease, and then sent it hurtling towards the window she herself was watching from. Wynter shrieked and clambered away, but luckily the exterior of the house took the force of his attack and the three captive housemates were kept safe, for now.

He was testing the forces holding them safely inside. Seeing what could cross over and what couldn't. This clearly was not a hostage negotiation, but a mission for vengeance, casualties be damned.

Wynter turned to Jakob with wide eyes and she climbed into his open arms, finding shelter there, and solace. He held her like he just might love her back. As if he were scared of losing her. Or at least she hoped so.

It would be nice to die thinking someone actually did

love her.

"I can't let him hurt you," she whispered.

"And I cannot let him take you away. Not now," Jakob answered, and Wynter turned her head so she could peer up into his face. She was about to ask what he'd meant by that, when she saw his eyes begin to change their hue. The incredible blues were resonating with waves of light and dark from deep within.

The sight was mesmerising, and she knew exactly what it meant. Jakob's soul was screaming to hers, and he wasn't even trying to hide it.

"So you did lie to me after all," she whispered, stroking his cheek tenderly as she watched his eyes glow brighter still. "You do have a soul."

"Apparently so," he replied with a soft smile, his gaze still boring into hers. And she didn't look away, not even for a second.

"What now?" Wynter asked, thinking they were quickly running out of time, and options.

"Come here," he said, holding her closer, and she couldn't deny that she wanted it. Wanted him. Unlike all the times when Marcus's eyes had shone like this, she craved the soul on offer behind the eyes currently staring into her own.

There was no denying that she loved him. No refusing his call, or that pull he had.

"No," Camilla shouted, and she tried to grab them and yank the pair apart, but it was no use. They both ignored her.

Wynter continued to peer back into Jakob's eyes and realised that what she felt wasn't about sex or the intimacy, but the comfort and the adoration she felt for him. And the love resonating between the two of them. It was real and unbreakable, and as she continued to stare into his impossibly bright eyes, Wynter accepted the vampire before her.

His soul reached for hers and she let it. The good

and the bad, none of it mattered. All that existed was them, and Wynter realised then how she was already free. That she loved Jakob and was ready to accept whatever lay ahead, just as long as they were together.

Her soul merged with his in that moment of clarity and acceptance. It felt like some kind of explosion in her chest, and was terrifying, but even when each of them realised what was happening, neither tried to stop it.

Jakob then kissed her fervently and smiled, watching her bask in his affection as they both ignored the world around them for a few seconds and performed the strange and unbreakable rite.

They were one now. Two halves of a whole and, against all odds, they truly loved one another.

She'd never been happier and felt her entire body ache for him.

Wynter had to admit, she didn't feel much different in herself afterwards, but she could see a difference in Jakob. The way he touched her and was aware of her every movement told her he had some instinctual need to keep watch over her. To have her close and safe, and even when Camilla approached them, he bristled and put himself between his sire and his soul mate.

"You don't speak to her, Camilla. Don't look at her. Don't try and hurt her. Not any more," he demanded. "She's mine."

"I can see that," Camilla retorted with a sour look on her face, "but have you stopped to think what Marcus is going to make of this happy little union? I doubt he'll accept it, even if he has no hope of coming between the two of you."

"We will fight," Wynter answered resolutely.

"Then you will die, and so will Jakob," she countered, but then her features softened.

Camilla took a proper look at the vampire she herself had sired, and sighed. She touched Jakob's face with her hand and shook her head, marvelling at the change in him. "Or I can help you."

"How?" both she and him answered at the same time and Camilla smiled to herself.

"I shall require Wynter's blood. And then, you two must jump," she told them, pointing to the back door that led directly out onto the cliff edge. Wynter couldn't fathom what she was getting at, but Jakob seemed to understand and he nodded.

"Thank you," he told her, before rushing to the kitchen.

He then returned with a knife and an empty mug. "Let me take some, just a little…" he asked Wynter, and took her hand in his. She nodded, watching as he ever so delicately cut her wrist and let the blood flow into the cup he'd held at the ready.

She felt like asking him why, but instead just accepted that what he was doing was for the best. Something deep within told her not to question Jakob's actions, and for once, she went along with what was happening and had no argument at all.

After wrapping the wound to close it, Jakob then gave the cup to Camilla with a nod. She drank it down and, without a backwards glance, walked directly out into the front garden towards her awaiting foes.

"She's sacrificing herself for you," Wynter realised, "but why me?"

"Because we are one, Wynter," Jakob replied with a frown, "and now, we must run. There isn't much time."

Wynter nodded and, without daring to look back in Marcus's direction, she followed Jakob towards the cliff edge and let him lift her onto his back. Once secured, she held tight and closed her eyes.

"Do it," she whimpered, and then felt the rush of air whizz past as Jakob stepped off and the pair of them went plummeting towards the rocky ground.

TWENTY

Marcus sensed so very many changes happening around him, and could smell Wynter on the air even still, but her scent had altered. Her lingering presence was gone and only a part of her remained. He wasn't sure what it meant, but something suddenly felt wrong.

And then, all of a sudden, a figure stepped out of the nothingness and appeared like an apparition in the morning sunlight. It was Camilla, and she reeked of Wynter's scent. So, that answered at least one of his questions, but as Marcus approached her, he realised just why she smelled so strongly of his beloved girl. She had tasted her. Drank from her.

"You dare drink from my slave?" he roared as he advanced, pinning Camilla by her throat and taking her down onto the ground. "I thought you'd agreed not to hurt her?"

"I lied," Camilla replied, mocking him with a deep belly laugh that made his blood boil, "I drank her dry and then left her to rot. Jakob too. He was weak and refused to kill her for me, so I took care of them both."

"I don't believe it," Marcus roared, but then he searched for any other sign of her, and realised Camilla was right. He couldn't smell her or sense Wynter like before. The only lingering presence was the scent of her blood on the vampire in his grasp's lips, and for that, he ripped her head clean from her shoulders.

She was dead in an instant and yet Marcus was still left unsatisfied. He needed to see the body. To know for sure that Wynter was gone. He turned to his horde and issued another of his silent commands.

Find a way in.

Failing that, you find whoever is responsible for this cloaking spell and break it.

He had to know the truth and see it with his own eyes. Marcus couldn't rest until he knew that she was dead. That he would never see her alive again. If it were true, he wouldn't rest easy, but at least he'd be able to move forward. Move on.

His Priestess was going to tell him more about what she'd divined. And maybe tell him off. Had she seen this coming? Was all of this part and parcel of the prophecy she had delivered? The full moon has risen after all and it was possible Wynter had done as Marcella had foreseen and gone into the arms of another. But who?

Warren was miles away and Jakob wasn't capable of love. Camilla herself had told him how her progeny was soulless so it couldn't be him.

Either way, he had to know the truth, and quickly.

He'd had enough of the guessing games.

***

Wynter and Jakob hit the rocky ground with a hard thud and she almost lost her grip on him it was so thundering. The shock of it was still reverberating around in her bones as she righted herself, but he didn't seem fazed in the slightest by the fall. She peered up at where they'd dropped from and couldn't quite believe they'd fallen so far without injury, and held Jakob tighter as it dawned on her just how much trouble they were in.

Marcus was going to find them. And when he did, Jakob was all but dead. Wynter wanted to weep. What had they done? Such fools, the pair of them. There was no doubt about it. They'd have to be clever and cunning if they had any hope of evading her oppressive boss, and she didn't even know where to begin.

"Jak, where can we go? What can we do?" she whispered in his ear, but rather than answer her, he put her down and turned to her with a frown.

"It's already too late," he told her, stroking her cheek with his hand. And then he placed a soft kiss against her lips. "They've found us."

"Who?" Wynter asked, but she got her answer before her soul mate could utter another sound.

Everything suddenly went still and eerily silent.

The wind came to a strange stop.

Even the waves seemed to take a step back, and that was when Wynter saw two unnervingly pale figures approaching from the corner of each eye. They were men, if she could call them that, and were advancing at breakneck speed, running directly towards them. "No. No. No," she muttered over and over, her head darting left and right as the vampire soldiers approached them. "What do we do, Jak?"

"Run!" Jakob screamed at her, shoving Wynter away, and she fell back on the sand just as the two soldiers collided with her beloved. The three of them began to fight, but then one of the soldiers stopped and turned to her, seemingly fixated on her scent as Wynter clambered back in fear. His deep, red eyes burned into her soul and then the vampire approached, his hands reaching out.

Wynter screamed and cried out as his icy hand touched her, assuming she would be dead a second later, but instead the vampire pulled her to him, his mouth open as if he were about to take a bite.

She pushed her hands against his huge shoulders and

punched at him in vain, which was when she noticed how the beaded bracelet on her wrist was now somehow fully white. The black bead was gone, but the bracelet hadn't been broken. It was somehow still fully intact.

And that was when she felt the presence of another being beside them. The vampire holding her was then suddenly wrenched back by hands that were as black as the bead had once been. As he was thrown, Wynter caught proper sight of her strange saviour. It was clearly a man, but he wasn't like anyone she'd seen before. His body was wispy, like it might not really be there, and yet he was fighting the vampire soldier with ease as if he were whole. He was laying punches against his pale skin that caused blows as real as Jakob's were against the other soldier.

She could do nothing more than watch in shock as they continued to fight around her. Was this the protection the Priestess had told her about? No, surely it couldn't be? Wynter was sure she had to be overthinking things. Perhaps even seeing things in her shock. The bracelet was nothing more than a trinket. The man was just dark skinned and moving so fast she couldn't see him properly.

Yeah, and the two zombie-like soldiers embroiled in battles before her were just men.

Not to mention her vampire soul mate.

God, she really was fucked.

She continued to watch and it truly seemed as if the soulless vampire killer who had grabbed her was no match for his new foe, and so Wynter left them to battle it out and focussed her attention back on Jakob. He was miraculously still alive and fighting the other soldier off, but it was clear his strength was waning, and Wynter decided she had to intervene.

These soldiers were Marcus's lackeys after all, and so she had to assume they weren't there to kill her, but to take her back as a hostage. Unharmed. With Jak, on the other hand, she was willing to bet there were no such caveats.

She saw the soldier rear back and then flung herself between them, and took the punch meant for Jakob directly to her collarbone, which snapped in two like a twig. She screamed in pain, but didn't regret it. The vampire stopped for the merest second to assess the situation, and Wynter used it as her chance to save Jakob's life.

There was no end of pain radiating from her broken bone, but Wynter's body also flooded with much needed adrenaline and she used every ounce of strength she had left to climb back on her feet and face the vampire soldier nose-to-nose.

"You have one real objective, am I right? To take me to your master," she demanded of him and was answered with a sneer. "Then do it," Wynter added, before taking off in the direction of the dunes ahead.

She didn't get far before the soldier was on her, of course, but she managed to look back and saw Jakob had been left behind, just like she'd planned. He was still kneeling in the sand, watching her in shock. "Run you idiot!" she then bellowed, and was pleased to see him follow her order.

Jak stood and charged directly into the ocean in a bid to escape before either soldier noticed her ruse, taking the one and only chance she was able to offer him.

He turned back for a second to shout to her before he let the waves carry him away, and as the soldier finally took her down, Wynter held onto Jakob's words like gospel.

I'll save you...

The end of book two in the Blood Slave series...

BLOOD SLAVE: ROUND TWO

ABOUT THE AUTHOR

Eden Wildblood is a new author, setting out on a journey to tell her dark stories to the world. She devours horror movies and books, and listens to heavy metal, and yet always wonders why people are still surprised when she reveals her dark side.

But now, she's using that part of herself to bring that darkness to life. To share her soul with the world…

Find out more about Eden by following her on Facebook:

www.facebook.com/edenwildblood

Printed in Poland
by Amazon Fulfillment
Poland Sp. z o.o., Wrocław